The

THE GROWTH

Adam Hulse

Cover by Laura Cathart
IG: @cutfingers

The Growth

A Message from Damien Casey, An Asshole

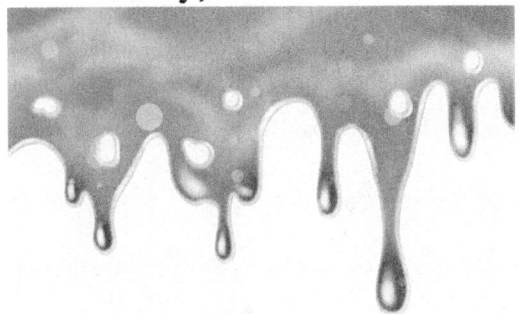

I really want to start this with some really cool story about meeting Adam and being blown away by how talented he is upon laying eyes on him. Something about how we met in a jungle hunting for some elusive cryptid; neither of us trying to hurt it, just find proof. But! We would also not be proving it to the world because we wouldn't want to do that to the cryptid.

So, I met Adam Hulse in the middle of a hostile and dangerous jungle in which we were both searching for a cryptid. The jungle is Twitter, the cryptid is being taken seriously as a writer. Adam and I have both struggled with either a genuine realization or an anxiety driven one that says, "no one takes you assholes seriously; you know that right?" We would talk for lengthy exchanges about this exact thing; and we still do.

I believe one of us followed the other

The Growth

and then the other followed back; we kept following each other instead of doing that thing some people do where they wait a week and unfollow you for the numbers; I'm looking at you guy who only has a bed and a guitar amp. I know the catalyst for that follow was Sarah Jane Huntington. She may not know it, but having her as a mutual friend is like being related to someone. If your friends with Sarah Jane, you know this: she keeps you close, she's always there when you need to talk or be hyped up, and she's just a fantastic person. Sarah deserves a thank you in this because I wouldn't have met a great friend and phenomenal writer named Adam Hulse without her.

Now let me type a bunch of true shit about Adam that I'm sure you'll think I'm saying because he's my friend.

Adam Hulse fucking rules.

You're going to find that out in the next 100+ pages.

The Growth duology is what I would call part of Adam's "Pre-Open Your Eyes" era. An example of that would be pre-It King or pre Great and Secret Show Barker. Works that show the beggining of the writer's trademark writing voice. It's an AFI reference, the album Shut Your Mouth and Open Your Eyes is a classic AFI album for sure, but it is one where their signature sound wasn't completely and totally developed. Thats what you have here with The Growth.

The Growth

The Growth Duology is a back to back kick in the teeth about a... nah, you're about to read it. What it shows about Adam is a developing voice. A voice that is pissed off about the state of the world around him, but also really wants to write huge scale horror about monsters.

Hulse writes two tales about a lack of government give a shit and exploitation. Hulse is never once afraid to shy away from a harsh critique of society in his writing; look at Beyond Economic Thresholds for proof.

There is a scene in another of Adam's books that shows the main character taking an elevator to the top floor of the building ran by the assholes who are making poor people poorer and more miserable. The character's focus is drawn to a Nirvana song that has been changed into elevator music. This scene is the quintessential Adam Hulse for me. We've spent pages upon pages with the character; we feel the same triumph he does as we know by the flow of story, and the amount of pages left, an end is coming. This scene summarizes the entirety of the book in the most perfect way Hulse could.

Here's a song by a band that had the image and presentation of relating to us, the underprivileged. A pissed off band making loud music to get under the skin of the people who continuously take from them. The use of their song is just one more notch on the disrespect bedpost. These people have not only made our lives miserable, but now theyve turned our music into a cheap novelty that barely passes as entertainment.

This is the world Hulse creates in his writing, and this is the world you're going to find in The Growth duology. It's harsh, cold, angry, and bitter. That doesn't mean it's hopeless though. With every bleak tale Hulse writes, there is hope. Hope for a better future for his characters and all of us. THAT is the true world of Hulse; one where no matter what ugliness we face, there can be hope... or we all die at the hands of some weird melty shit. Either way works for me.

The Growth

The Near Future

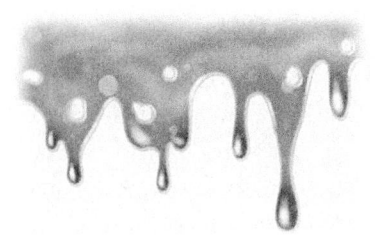

Smoke rose from the north where the church of St. George still burned. The fifty or so known survivors on Ithaki Island gathered on Amoudaki beach, exchanging looks of terror and nervousness. There were only enough boats for around thirty people and the tension clung to the air like fog. They had agreed to attempt the short crossing en masse in a desperate bid to make it to Kakoghilos beach, which lay in wait on the larger island of Kefalonia. The breakthrough made in England was slowly fighting back, but help was always slow to reach smaller islands. They prayed things would be a little better at their destination simply because it couldn't get any worse. Artemis stood waiting for her husband, Kostas and drummed her fingers on the kayak she was guarding on the sand. A bare-chested man in his late fifties made no attempt to hide his interest in the couple's means of escape, and Artemis found herself craning her neck to get a better view of her partner.

Kostas was talking as animatedly as

possible for someone in the throes of starvation to the newly installed leader, Georgios. The short, balding man was quick to anger, which was apparently enough to grant one a place of authority in these crazy times. Even now, Artemis could see Georgios furrow his single eyebrow at Kostas. She also noticed her topless observer had inched a little closer across the sand. Artemis produced a thin-bladed weapon from her waistband and let the sun catch its steel. The man clenched his jaw before retreating behind a nearby family. Artemis viewed this group with something nearing amazement.

How is it possible to keep children living with all this going on? she thought.

Kostas stormed to her side.

"Unbelievable," he spat.

"What is wrong?"

"That idiot, Georgios, is going to let any boat with an engine go first."

Artemis's heart sank. The amount of noise it would create in the water would surely mean those in kayaks and other rowing boats would be left totally vulnerable. They had all known, of course, what this plan really meant, hadn't they? Not safety in numbers, but a lottery of life and death. If any of them made it across then it would surely be because the others had rushed to watery graves.

"We have no choice," Artemis simply told her husband.

The Growth

Kostas nodded and stroked his beard in a way that his wife knew he did when he was nervous. Artemis turned away from the gaunt person who had somehow replaced the big strong love of her life and prayed there would be some means of nourishment on Kefalonia.

Small groups of men stood with hands on hips or shielding their eyes as they looked out to sea. Artemis knew they searched for the tell-tale darkness, but it was hard to be sure when the lonely sun shimmered off every watery movement. One thing was obvious, though. For the last three days, there appeared to be a section of clear water from one island to the other, which meant there was finally a slim chance they could leave the unspeakable carnage behind them.

There was a commotion from the group at the front of the gathering as the four small boats with engines were dragged toward the sea. All these surviving boats had been frantically pulled from the water when the last remaining ferry had been attacked from below. Artemis had meant to help but had found herself hypnotised by the way the ferry had shuddered and lurched from side to side. The screams had seemed far away yet close by. A cruel trick, the last which the waves had control of. The ferry had long since been pulled to the cold depths, but Artemis looked at the last spot she had seen the vessel before it sank along with fifty-five souls.

The Growth

Now, the small boats bobbed peacefully on the calm waters of the shallows while their owners looked at each other in wonderment and cagey optimism. There was a brief moment of silence before pandemonium broke out. A middle-aged couple rushed toward the nearest boat but were shot in their backs as they waded forward. Georgios began barking threats at the masses and even wasted a bullet of his own by firing over the crowd. A fight erupted near Artemis, and she watched in horror as a knife-wielding trio attacked a young couple for refusing to give up their inflatable dinghy. The end result was the couple lying face down in the sand next to their punctured salvation. All three whistled the last of their air onto the beach. It was one of the many wasteful episodes Artemis had witnessed which she forced herself to put in a lockbox in the back of her mind.

Artemis looked toward the boats where the two bodies bobbed their way back toward the sand as the sea looked to reject them. Georgios and his men had given up trying to restore order and were now helping each other clamber aboard the utility dinghies, which were the envy of all that watched on. One of Georgios' men was overcome by part of the mob, who held him under water but anyone who got close to one of the boats was dropped by a bullet or two. A child cried somewhere, but Artemis couldn't see where they were as

The Growth

panicked adults ran in all directions. She looked out to sea and thought she saw a flicker of darkness there, yet it seemed to be swallowed up by the glare from the sun. Only when she turned to mention this to Kostas did she realise her husband had already dragged their kayak near the water's edge. His progress only faltered when he realised he didn't have an oar. Artemis looked at her feet where the two oars lay and then back at Kostas, who was shouting at her to hurry.

The sound of outboard motors mingled in the air with the occasional gunshot and plea for help. Artemis was two metres from Kostas when she was grabbed from behind. She didn't need to turn to know it was the bare-chested man who had been watching her so closely. Artemis dropped one of the oars but gripped the other as the man's arms reached around so his hands could join hers there. The man grunted and his breath was warm and stale on her neck, motivating Artemis to push her exhausted body so she could struggle even more violently.

"Give it," he huffed.

Artemis clenched her teeth and tried to throw her elbows into the man's stomach, but she felt as though she were fighting in a dream, and her blows were ineffective. Kostas dropped the kayak so he could rush to her, and Artemis felt a flicker of warmth in her heart.

You're in for it now, old man, she thought.

The Growth

The love drained from her like the last of the rainwater they had collected two days earlier. Kostas, the love of her life, didn't even look at her as he scooped up the fallen oar and ran back to the kayak.

"Don't leave me," Artemis begged as she wrestled with the older man.

Kostas did not turn as he launched the kayak into the sea. He didn't even turn when a complete stranger jumped up and sat in Artemis's place before using his hands as a second oar. Artemis realised she was now clinging to a redundant item and let go of the oar. The man behind was too stupid to realise the fight was over, and Artemis found herself still trapped.

"He's gone," she said quietly.

"Give me the oar, bitch," the man cursed.

Artemis watched her husband make good progress ahead of the other motorless vessels. The love became infected with rage, and she could almost taste its bitterness in her dried-out mouth. Kostas was well out of reach, but the man who still attacked her passive body was not. Artemis threw her head back in a flurry of long black hair. There was a crunch from a broken nose, and the man released her as though she were suddenly on fire. Artemis turned to see crimson gushing over the man's bare chest. It ran until it caught in his grey hair.

"You broke my nose, you bitch!" he cried.

Artemis collected the oar and swung at the

The Growth

man, so it connected with his jaw. He staggered as though drunk, and Artemis chased him down with chops of the makeshift weapon. She didn't just see this vile man; she saw Kostas and every man who had done her wrong since puberty. Eventually the oar snapped, and the man fell to the sand with a whimper.

"Call me bitch again," she raged.

"Please," he begged through cowering hands.

Artemis pulled the knife from her waistband.

"Say *that* word again," she demanded.

The man began to cry, and Artemis took one last look at the sea before plunging the blade into the man's throat.

"Call me bitch again!" she screamed as she worked the knife in and out.

*

Kostas already felt his muscles burning from rowing and stared at the distant motorboats with an envy which was almost maddening. He refused to look back at the man who rowed with his hands, preferring to pretend it was Artemis sitting there. It was a betrayal which he would try and process once he had food and fresh water in his belly. There were two boats nearby who paddled along with him. One was an old wooden dinghy that had a grey-looking man struggling with long oars as

The Growth

four more people sat there unable to help like leeches to his efforts. One of these passengers was a boy of around twelve who stared at Kostas constantly with eyes that judged.

He knows what I've done, Kostas thought bitterly.

Rather than face up to the latest chapter of his nightmarish reality, Kostas robotically fixated on rowing.

Disaster reared its chaotic head while he was in this trance-like state. Distant gunshots and screams reached them from the boats which Georgios and his men had claimed. Two of the men were immediately taken. Kostas watched wide-eyed as what looked like a long black tendril emerged from the water and smashed a third boat in half in a hail of splinters and clouds of gore. Georgios sat in the remaining motorboat as it attempted to turn around and head back to Ithaki in failure. Those around Kostas saw the black water chasing Georgios toward them, and with cries of anguish they began to make their own adjustments to head back to shore. Kostas stopped rowing and sat dumbly watching the chase. He allowed himself to think of his wife and dropped the oar into the water.

"What the hell are you doing?" the man behind him screamed.

Kostas didn't answer nor turn around. His passenger began to strike him on the back but when he realised that Kostas would not be

The Growth

moved, he jumped into the sea and began a futile attempt at swimming away from the shadows that came for them.

Georgios and his men emptied their bullets into the mass, painfully aware that it was having no effect. Guns were only useful against human enemies. For a brief moment, there seemed to be enough clear sea between the rear engine and the dark shapes which danced through wood, skin, and bone. Georgios was just starting to believe they'd make it back to their desolate island when his boat became completely silent. He had to look back to realise the motor had been ripped cleanly from its housing. Kostas sat in his kayak not thirty metres from Georgios and the two men briefly exchanged knowing looks. Then a wave that defied the sea's movement appeared to the side of Georgios' boat like a wall of thick jet-black oil. It smashed down onto the occupants of the vessel and changed them to shaking skeletons. Kostas looked on in terror as clumps of flesh still clung there, steaming. Then the boat was pulled under, and the darkness came for him. He sobbed back fear as the green water changed to display impossible shapes which moved like prehistoric jellyfish. For a moment he thought he saw his own face looking back at him, but his trance was disturbed by a strange hissing sound. The kayak was dissolving and being absorbed into the mass. As Kotas' legs melted and fused into the

The Growth

sinking kayak, the black shapes passed by in pursuit of the swimming man and the other rowing boats. His life was already an afterthought.

*

The screams from the dozen onlookers on the beach almost matched the howls of agony from the sea. Artemis stepped away from the butchered corpse of the bare-chested man and looked out to watch the last rowing boat dragged violently down. For a little while the people on the beach milled around unsure what to do but when the shallows began to turn black, they instinctively retreated to higher ground. None of them approached the crazy blood-soaked women who's back still heaved from the demands of murder. Artemis looked at the fallen body of the man she had killed and reached down to drag it away from the beach. She was exhausted but every time she neared failure, she thought of Kostas leaving her behind which propelled her out of view of the crowd.

Artemis began to gather driftwood together so she could make a fire using a glass bottle and the last of the sun's rays. She ignored the bubbling black water and the swishing sounds that came from there. Artemis knew from experience she was out of reach and crouched near the fire she'd started on the

The Growth

scrub land. After an hour, she dragged the body of the man and carefully lowered his legs onto the glowing embers. The mission to reach Kefalonia had failed but at least she would eat tonight.

Jimmy (2022)

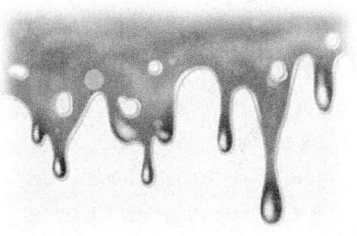

The two North-West water engineers sat on the opposite side of the closed off road to the four members of the ATS cleaning team. Although they had been toiling underground together for two days there was still the kind of awkward division humans liked to create when representing different teams. This didn't stop Jimmy from ATS being thoroughly disgusted with fellow team member Ste as the latter shoved the last of his bacon on toast into his mouth.

"How can you eat after being down there?"

"I didn't get it from down there though did I," Ste protested through the partially consumed mouthful of lunch.

Jimmy smirked as ketchup blobbed onto the man's overalls. Ste was the same age as Jimmy, but his excessive smoking and love of booze had put ten years on the thirty-six that he'd lived for.

"Shit!" Ste groaned at the spillage.

"No, shit is what we've been elbow deep

The Growth

in," Jimmy complained. "You've not even washed your hands."

"I was wearing gloves!"

"So what?"

Jimmy screwed up his face as he watched Ste scoop up the ketchup with his finger.

"Anyway," Ste grunted as he stood up into a stretch. "We've been elbow deep in a fatberg, not shit."

This brought laughter and shaking heads of disbelief from the rest of the ATS team.

"Have you heard this?" Jimmy turned to acknowledge their descent.

"What?" Ste threw his hands up after depositing a cigarette between his lips.

"What do you think is in a fatberg?"

"Erm, fat!"

"Yes genius, there is. As well as nappies and shit!"

Ste shrugged and made a point of rubbing his hand over his face before the laughter was pierced by a shrill whistle.

The PPE wrapped water engineers were already disappearing down the open sewage shaft with the familiar sound of boots hitting metal rungs.

"Do those pricks think we're dogs or something?" Ste complained as he looked around for his hard-hat.

This brought a series of guffaws from the cleaning team which continued until they were underground. The echoes it produced rendered

The Growth

the men self-conscious and the laughter faded. Jimmy stepped over the thick hoses which were bloated like hellish worms and waited for Ste to trip over them just like every other time so far.

"Shit!"

Jimmy smirked and then approached the fatberg with a frown. The high-pressure jets from the hoses were doing their job but there was still the matter of delivering the disgusting chunks of waste to the surface. From past experience they had brought a large plastic container and pulley system to remove the waste as they broke the fatberg down. Shovelling the hardened fat full of hand wipes and nappies was bad enough without having to carry it by hand. Jim approached the nearest water engineer who was standing with his hands on his hips looking at the blockage as though it were a personal attack on his family.

"If this had got any worse the houses up there would be swimming in filth."

"Ever seen one like this before, mate?"

Jimmy called everyone "mate" because he struggled to remember names. The nameless water engineer attempted to adjust his safety glasses, grew frustrated, and turned back to the mass of waste.

"One in London I did was the size of a bungalow."

Jimmy did a double-take due to the combination of information and the man's cockney accent he'd failed to notice previously. He was about to make more small talk, anything but return to the filth, when Ste jumped back from the area he had been chiselling at.

"Jesus Christ!"

Jimmy and the cockney watched on in confusion as Ste collided with Dave and Terry which threw up splashes of water and expletives.

"What's up with you?" Jimmy bellowed.

Ste didn't answer as he was too busy staring at the area of the fatberg he'd just jumped back from.

"Ste?"

Jimmy placed his hand tentatively on the man's shoulder who in turn recoiled in fear.

"Ste, what the hell's up with-?"

"It's breathing," Ste blurted out with a point of his chisel.

The tunnel was once more filled with laughter which bounced from surface to surface. Ste was red faced with the kind of anger only humiliation can evoke, and was just about to protest, when there was a strange sensation throughout the sewers.

Jimmy felt as though his skull was vibrating and was reminded of falling asleep with his head against the door in his Dad's car. He realised the vibration was working its way through his thick boots and into his bones.

"Everyone back," the cockney shouted.

The Growth

All of the team managed a few staggered steps in retreat before the frontal layers of the fatberg fell away in crumpled chunks. Every man cringed in anticipation of expected carnage, yet the vibrating ceased as did the falling debris.

"See," Ste bleated. "It's breathing!"

Jimmy couldn't quite understand what he was seeing. The fatberg had disappeared and in its place was a wall of black sludge which shimmered. He thought he detected a rise and fall in the mass but before he could be certain the vibrating started up again and the shape quivered sickeningly.

"What is *that*?"

No answer came. The men in the sewage system weren't even sure who had asked the question. Had they simply thought it? Once again, the vibration stopped, and Jimmy cringed at the way the aftershocks rippled through the slimy mass his team would now have to try and remove. The water jets spluttered to a stop and the group realised Alan, the other water engineer, must have returned to the surface. An unnerving new silence fell between them, but Jimmy, Ste, and the cockney water engineer managed a few tentative steps towards the mass. Shapes appeared to bulge just under the surface as though trying to break through the membrane. It was hypnotising to watch but a white object caught Jimmy's attention which caused him to

The Growth

steam up his safety glasses.

"Do you see that?" he asked as he tore them from his face.

The mass pushed the object closer as though answering the question and Jimmy saw the skeletal remains of a large rat. The bones began to fall into themselves through compression and Jimmy began to doubt it was a skeleton at all. A stench of burning decay puffed out from the blockage and those doubts evaporated as though steamed.

"Ste, did you see that?"

After no answer came his way, Jimmy looked to his right to see Ste was staring wide-eyed at the mass directly opposite him. A lump had emerged which stretched towards the men, giving the surface the appearance of latex.

"No," Ste said simply.

Feet shuffled all around and Jimmy realised all in the sewer were running for the ladders that would take them away from the strange sights they'd chanced upon.

"Ste, we need to go."

"No, it can't be."

Jimmy took a step backwards and left Ste transfixed with the developing shape in front of him.

"Ste, come on mate we need to get out of here."

The vibrating started again like a tremor and Jimmy marvelled as the solid mass appeared to become translucent like a large

The Growth

pool of water. Ripples multiplied in maddening circles until the shuddering stopped and the mass became black once more. No more than three feet away from Ste's face was a perfect replica of his head stretching out from the very black growth which confronted them.

"Jimmy?" was all Ste could muster through a quivering tone.

Before Jimmy had chance to reply, the clay-like impression of Ste punched straight through the real version's face. The remnants became a sludge which slopped into the shallow water behind them. Jimmy screamed at the sight. Ste's body somehow remained erect while the new slime version of his head sat on its shoulders while facing the wrong way. The mass swelled in what Jimmy could only compare to excitement as it grew closer to him. He staggered back and saw his old friend's body encased and consumed. The smell of something ripe being burned filled the tunnel. He couldn't watch any longer, knowing Ste's decapitated corpse would go the same way as the rats had done before it. Jimmy sobbed in retreat until his feet pinged on the metal rungs as he fled from the rapidly growing bundle of death.

The Growth

Tax, the Inevitable Man

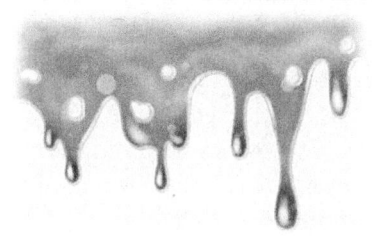

Lee Perkins couldn't recall when the nickname "Tax" had stuck, his memory was never kind to him, and he treated it with contempt as though it belonged to someone else. He'd asked once at the Black Rose pub, where he liked to drink coke and waste pound coins to bright flashing lights, but the answer had confused him. Big Dave laughed a belly laugh before his flabby face had grown stern like a mask.

"It's because you're inevitable, mate."

Tax had pretended to understand before searching the word out on the internet via his phone. For a short while he had forgotten the glowing machine near the bar as he pondered how the dictionary translation applied to his life. The only link he could make was when people asked him for help, he got things done. From then on, he accepted the nickname without question. If it meant he was helping, then that was ok with him.

Now though, he was walking through the damp streets of his estate with balled fists and

The Growth

a lump hammer sitting uncomfortably through his belt while he wondered if he was actually helping people at all. His niece had been hurt in a way his brother refused to talk about.

"It was that bastard Nicky Connor," was all he'd said on the matter.

The revelation was throwing Tax into a state of muddled confusion. He had helped Nicky recently with some squatters who had taken over one of his flats but now Nicky had hurt one of Taxs' family and it made no sense to him. Of course he knew Nicky was no angel, in fact Tax had also recently discovered the man's name was linked with the rising drug problem the area was suffering with.

Tax walked quickly through the rain with the hood from his sweater acting as an amateur disguise. His stocky build gave him away whenever he walked these streets. Today though, he needn't have been concerned as the grey broken pavements were deserted. Tax didn't even notice none of the usual modified cars sped down the back roads. It was oddly quiet, but not for Tax. All the inevitable man could hear was the tinnitus buzzing in his ears which intensified every time he thought of his niece's face. He loved his brother and his niece unconditionally and not being able to fully contribute to the house they shared had always been a source of shame. They told him not to worry about it, but he hated being anyone's burden. So if this was the best way to contribute right now, by God he was going to give it everything he had.

Tax looked up as a heavy thud of techno music followed the weed smoke out of the open windows. A large shape passed the frosted glass in the front door which got the soggy observers attention. Tax felt like a wet dog waiting to be let in by their owner. The thought amused him for a moment as he toyed with what breed he'd be. He liked to think he would be loyal and lovable but conceded he'd probably be vicious and quick to bite. Another flash of movement knocked Tax from his daydream, and he rushed to the front door. He was about to rattle it with his scarred fist when the loud music abruptly stopped. Tax watched his hand hover in front of the heavily weathered door. His plan had been to knock on the door and then force his way in once someone answered but the feeling his approach had been noticed was throwing him off. The large shape appeared on the other side of the frosted glass. Tax assumed this was Nicky's new enforcer his brother had warned him about.

"Be careful, he's a horrible bastard," he'd been told.

"So am I, brother," Tax had quietly replied.

The large shape moved to within inches of the glass.

"What do you want?"

The Growth

Although muffled, the tone was deep and full of threat and Tax ran over his brother's words once more.

"I wanna see Nicky," Tax steamed up a small circle on the glass.

"He's out."

Tax looked up at the bedroom window still bleeding smoke even though the chaotic tunes had ceased.

"I wanna see Nicky."

There was a muffled complaint from the top of the stairs and the large shape sprang into action. The door was unlocked and ripped open by a steroid fuelled giant who wore a tiny white vest to better frame his network of muscles. Nicky's new enforcer was a specimen of intimidation with the eyes of a reptile.

"Piss off before you get hurt, yeah?"

Tax had never been physically intimidated in his life. For him, it may as well have been something happening to a fish in the ocean. He turned as though to leave, but then quickly reached for the lump hammer. Just as he had rehearsed in the mirror, Tax delivered the blow in the same movement. The huge man's right knee cracked and dislocated. Tax watched in quiet satisfaction as large shaking hands reached for the afflicted joint only to realise it had moved to the side. The enforcer attempted to put his weight on the injured leg, howled, and fell backwards into the house.

Tax didn't bother shutting the front door

The Growth

behind him. He stepped over the sobbing man.

"Why did you do it Nicky?"

His voice sounded weary on the way up the stairs. Tax was near the top when a painfully skinny man in a tracksuit ran into the bathroom and locked the door. It wasn't Nicky, so Tax continued onto the landing where he could see the drug dealer sitting on a throne of stolen goods. Tax stopped on the metal threshold between one soiled carpet and another. Nicky was clutching a sword which reminded Tax of a film he'd watched with his dad.

What was it called?

Nicky scratched his short beard and sneered with annoyance.

"You must be mad coming in here like this."

Tax thought on this for a moment before producing a lazy shrug.

"I am mad," he said simply.

There was the first sign of distress from the big bad drug dealer. It was only a slight flicker of doubt in his eyes, but Tax had seen it there all the same.

"Is this about Sue?"

Tax took a step into the stale bedroom.

"I think you need more muscle," he said with a jab to indicate downstairs.

Nicky brightened at this as though a great plan had been formulated.

"Well why don't you come and work for

me again?"

Tax took another step closer to conflict.

"Plenty of money, Tax. You won't need to play on the gamblers anymore."

Tax heard the desperation now as well.

"I like playing on the gamblers."

Nicky closed his eyes for a moment before waving the thin sword in the air.

"That bitch had it coming!"

Anger was the last desperate ploy, even Tax knew that. Like a dog barking one last time to ward off an attacker.

I wonder what type of dog I'd be?

There was an inhuman scream from the bathroom. It was a sound so deeply unsettling that it halted the drama in the bedroom immediately.

"Gaz?" Nicky shouted over Taxs' shoulder.

The answer was a furious, thumping against the inside of the bathroom door. Nicky and Tax exchanged a look of concern.

"Are we going to check or are you going to stand there with your hammer?"

Tax was off guard. The plan had followed the smoke out of the open bedroom window and now his body felt too warm again. He would take a swipe of Nicky's sword over a direct question any day of the week. There was another scream from the bathroom, but this one was more muffled than the last as though Gaz was choking on something.

The Growth

Nicky dashed past Tax before the latter could react or clear the fog from his mind. The sound of the bathroom door breaking apart shook Tax from his confusion, so he quickly joined Nicky on the landing. The men forgot their conflict as they strained their eyes and minds in an attempt to comprehend what had happened in the bathroom. It looked like the toilet had exploded and sent forth a display of strange fluids and slime.

"What the fuck?" Nicky gasped.

Tax didn't respond as he was too busy drinking in the spectacle before him. His eyes took big gulps of the fluctuating shapes slowly emerging from the smashed ceramic of the toilet. One part was stretched up like a barbed vine and it held Gaz around his blueish grey neck. Nicky looked at the man's body as it shuddered for the last time. He marvelled at the man who was being held two feet from the bare floorboards. The mass slopped over the sides of the bowl and up the dirty tiles to become the very room into which it had sneaked. Yet still more emerged as though it would never end. One of the dead man's fallen trainers began to melt as it was encased in the strange slime. The men wouldn't have noticed if it hadn't fizzed as the mess consumed it.

Nicky was the first to break and bolted for the stairs. He tried to skirt the banister, so he was as far away from the entrance to the bathroom as possible. It wasn't far enough

The Growth

though. The ooze that had previously moved so laboriously, quickly burst into life. It dropped the smoking corpse it held and snapped out two long hardened lengths of itself which wrapped firmly around Nicky's ankles. With one thrust the screaming man was brought crashing, facedown, onto the top of the staircase. The impact sent his sword halfway down the escape he was so desperately close to.

"Tax, help me!"

A quick lesson was learned, and Tax hurdled the rail, so he landed painfully just five steps down from Nicky's screaming face.

"Help me, please!" he begged.

Tax looked at Nicky's knuckles that were almost glowing white with the effort of holding onto the top step. His desperate face was already bright red with the effort of not being dragged back into the bathroom. Tax shook his head once which sent Nicky into a meltdown.

"You stupid, thick bastard!" he roared.

Tax had heard it all before and was about to turn away when Nicky had one last thing to say.

"Sue says it about you too!"

The words meant nothing to Tax. He knew Sue would never say that about him. What triggered Tax was the smirk that played on Nicky's lips at the mention of her name. Even now as death burned and pulled at him, he showed what he really was. Tax drew back

The Growth

the hammer because sometimes a smirk was all it took, and pulverised the skull just above Nicky's shocked eyes. The moment he let go of the stairs Nicky was dragged quickly from sight.

Tax took a few steps to freedom before he collided with Nicky's injured enforcer. Somehow the big man had managed to drag his bulky frame halfway up the stairs. They noticed Nicky's sword as one and stretched for it. Tax wasn't quick enough, and the enforcer brought the sword up so he could drive it down like a stake. It was the only available technique to use in such close quarters. Tax had to drop his hammer so he could grab at the man's large wrists. He was pressed against one wall while the enforcer leaned over him. Tax moved to the side as the sword wavered an inch away from his face. The staircase was filled with the sounds produced by man since their primitive ancestors first began battling. Grunts and laboured breathing of two people trying to kill each other. Tax was moments from begging for mercy. Seconds away from telling his attacker about what lurked upstairs when the enforcer's damaged knee slipped from the step. The pair rolled heavily against each other as they bounced down the remaining steps. Tax closed his eyes to the washing machine sensation until he sprawled free of his opponent. There was a garbled gagging sound and when Tax looked to the bottom of the

The Growth

staircase, he saw the sword had entered the enforcer's mouth and was glistening red out of the back of his head.

Tax sat up just as a crescendo of noise and movement breached the staircase. He looked in horrified awe at the monstrous wave pouring over the carpet, carrying two half melted bodies with it. Tax scurried up to his feet just as the mass collided with the prone enforcer's back. There was no time to watch in engrossed horror as the thing from the bathroom poured across the hall. Tax fled the house and ensured he slammed the door shut this time, for what it was worth. He ran until the burning in his lungs reduced him to a quitter. Tax bent over double trying to get his breath back and process what had happened at Nicky's place. The unmistakable sound of sirens approaching at speed shocked the air.

Oh God, I've killed a man.

Tax turned in resignation, but the wailing cars barrelled past and out of sight. There was silence for a few heartbeats and then the screaming started.

Kevin

The television was seldom a thing of interest to Kevin. Maybe the technology of the device but not the endless nonsense it projected. Today was an exception. The breaking news had at first caused a break in his soldering work before completely absorbing his interest. Even though there was a nearby chair, Kevin had stood for forty-two minutes with his thin arms folded against his bony chest. The bright white teeth of the newsreader opened and shut rapidly as she recapped the situation to any viewers getting to the news alert later than others.

"-water services informed local police of the death of two members of the ATS Cleaning Services team who were assisting with a routine call-out. The area was immediately shut down while officers awaited the arrival of a specialist unit to deal with what they officially deemed to be a chemical spill. However, before they arrived, we received unconfirmed reports that the lives of two police officers were lost. One bystander claimed they witnessed one of the officers being dragged down through

The Growth

the sewers access point. As you can see from these aerial images, the exclusion zone was extended significantly as local business owners and residents were told to evacuate the area."

The live feed cut to a street level shot and Kevin noted the presence of armed police that were briefly caught on camera near a ribbon of police tape which danced in the breeze as though excited.

"As you can see the well protected team, equipped to deal with chemical spills, are on the scene now as they make their way to the centre of the exclusion zone. Ok right, we have this just in. We've obtained some mobile phone footage from the initial emergency situation. Presumably from a member of the team working in the waste system. We must warn you that viewers may find some of the following images distressing."

Kevin watched as shaky footage showed men in waterproof overalls flinging themselves out of the underground access point. He wondered how many lives had been lost because a person's first thought was to get their phone out and start filming the drama. The sound cut in and out as though the person shooting the footage was clutching their phone too tightly. Each person that emerged wore the same mask of terror. It reminded Kevin of survivors being dug out of ruins or staggering away from an act of terrorism. Horrified faces

The Growth

full of shock shambled past the camera as the phone holder moved back to the opening in the road.

"Where's Ste?" someone screamed off camera.

The camera is held over the gap, but the camera loses focus before the viewers see the desperate and agonised efforts of another uniformed man attempting to climb the ladder. He holds his hand out towards the screen and then is suddenly snapped from sight. There is a brief glimpse of a blue gloved hand gripping around one of the ladder rungs and Kevin gasps when he realises the arm is no longer attached. He can only assume the news network was in too much of a hurry to release the footage to adequately censor the violence.

The news cut back to the studio where the tan colour has slightly drained from the newsreader's face. She taps at a few keys on her keyboard to regain her composure. Kevin doesn't hear what she has to say next as he throws hardware catalogues, computer magazines, and final notice warning letters in all directions in a desperate searches for the remote control. On finding it, he hits the rewind button to return to the mobile phone footage. Kevin waits for the moment the man is still on the ladder and hits the pause button. His arthritic thumb clicks along as he rapidly presses on the control to edge the image forward. It takes a while, but he catches the moment when a dark object enters the frame. Kevin stops pressing the button for a moment as he takes a step towards his television. He squints as what at first looked like a jet of water now seems to be solid and lance shaped.

"What the hell?"

Kevin begins to move the image forward and almost cringes for the man on the ladder as the lance inches closer and closer. At the moment of contact there is a further shadow from the left of the screen where the lance shape emerged from. Once again, Kevin stops pressing the button and moves even closer to the screen.

"What is *that?*"

Within the mass where the lance has emerged from there is a shiny white orb. It could be a reflection from the street above, but Kevin has other ideas. In his opinion it's the malevolent eye of a strange creature.

Breathless, he presses stop on the controller, so the television returns to a live broadcast. Kevin is infuriated by the sight of reality television stars progressively losing their clothing during an advertisement for the latest debacle.

"Circus." he mutters as he walks through the mazes of boxes which have taken over his home.

Returned stock from his latest failed invention and the final straw for his now ex-girlfriend Deborah. The image on the box is of

The Growth

a smiling jogger wearing glow in the dark running shoes. Even though early testing had been positive enough to get his patent manufactured, all early reviews were damning in their response to the fact that after twenty minutes the running shoe began to heat up. Turns out the last thing runners want is to feel warmer than exercise is already getting them. Kevin looked at the circuit board he had been soldering and sighed. He didn't need to be rich; he just needed enough money to allow him to return to his favoured field of chemistry.

The chemical spill angle on the news had piqued his interest because he had one such invention he believed could be a massive help to the emergency services and put his name on a more favourable footing. He turned from his boxes of failures and tapped a few keys on his laptop to gain access to his favoured science forum. Had they seen the eye?

N00b79 : Are you seeing this?
dRfeelGood : Worlds gone mad.
RaVEn : Doesn't sound like a chemical spill to me! What kind of chemical drags people to their deaths?
MrBits12 : (Tinfoil hat intensifies)
dRfeelGood : LOLZ
KevinEleven : Guys I think RaVEn is right. I've just been watching the mobile phone footage and whatever grabbed that guy is alive!

The Growth

MrBits12 : Grabbed?? He fell in!

dRfeelGood : Can I have some of what you two have been smoking?!

RaVEn : Oh he fell in and immediately disappeared in a blink of an eye? Yeah sure!

N00b79 : mobile phone footage?

MrBits12 : YES RaVEn!! Because he got swept away! IT'S CALLED WATER PRESSURE!

KevinEleven : i freeze framed and there was an eye

dRfeelGood : Where???

MrBits12 : Oh ffs!

RaVEn : Where did you see the eye mate?

KevinEleven : in the mass that snatched the man off the ladder

dRfeelGood : HAHAHAHAHAHAHAHAHA

MrBits12 : Jesus! Lol

RaVEn : leave him alone guys

Kevin quickly closed the lid on his laptop. Ridicule had followed him his whole life, but it never stopped stinging. It didn't matter if he was right or not, people still openly mocked his theories and inventions. There had been better times of course, back when he worked in the science wing of the military testing sector. He'd had some success at finding ways of combating dangerous toxins and a rare success in love when Deborah had enjoyed his clumsy advances. However, his failure had been catastrophic. Kevin had pitched his new chemical concoction to his superiors as a versatile defender against dirty bombs and chemical incidents. The concept of a small amount of this liquid being able to absorb and consume copious amounts of harmful products had granted the upcoming scientist an audience with his superiors. Kevin's solution had absorbed the staged chemical spill and the metal drum it had come from and he felt like bursting with pride at the nods of satisfaction from all in attendance. The feeling soon turned to a giddy freefall as the solution became unstable, ate through the floor, and severely burned two technicians in the laboratory below. The fallout had been swift. Kevin lost his job, pension, and was blacklisted from experimental sector for life. Deborah had stayed with him out of what Kevin now understood was pity, but even that was lost now.

The news returned with hurried updates regarding a spread in the incidents relating to the underground situation. Shots of emergency services struggling with panicked crowds was overdubbed with a sombre commentary regarding an unconfirmed death toll. Kevin fought the urge to go back to the forum just to tell his mockers to "suck it!" Instead he climbed around boxes until he was near a chest

The Growth

of drawers so he could put a jumper over his Tool t-shirt. He looked at the mirror on the wall above and tutted before flattening his greasy brown hair and retying his ponytail. Kevin gave a thin-lipped smile from under a ratty moustache and adjusted his glasses.

"Like polishing a turd," he told the lonely house.

His hand fished around in the top drawer in search of something other than worn out boxer shorts. Kevin retrieved a moleskin journal tightly bound by elastic bands. He didn't need to check inside to know the elaborate chemical formula for his biggest failure was scribbled in there. Kevin threw it in his bag with some more of his belongings before grabbing his wallet, phone, and keys. Items he'd never need again. Kevin was soon out in the fresh air for the first time in days. The sound of distant sirens carried to him, and he pulled his coat around him with a shiver. He could fix this; he just knew it.

Panic On the Streets

The reports of further incidents flooded in and eventually drowned the emergency services. Stretched thin from brutal budget cuts they toiled away until the need to find and hold their own families grew too strong. NHS nurses triaged from their own living rooms until entire streets caved in as the monster below cut straight through foundations. The strange alien-like mass devoured anyone unfortunate enough to be near a point of access. Loved ones were broken apart and dragged down through toilets and pets were devoured by a monster both small enough to fit through taps yet big enough to appear unstoppable. What at first seemed like dozens of separate incidents was soon realised to be acts performed by the same creature.

A hellish carnivorous beast which was spreading underground like damp in a dilapidated basement was soon nicknamed "the Growth" by the media who shared projected maps of ruin. The horrific events which started in the North-West of England

The Growth

were soon being repeated in the Midlands and the North-East. Men of science were dragged in front of TV cameras to argue with men of religion. What was this beast and where did it come from? Of course, the government urged calm from their hiding places while large communities became as lawless as the wild west. Mobs attacked supermarkets until they were worthless as society showed itself for what it really was. The similarity between man and the creature which was endlessly feeding was not lost on many, just simply ignored.

Thousands had lost their lives by the time the military were mobilised. Tanks and artillery were rendered useless by the movements of the Growth so brave units from the Royal Engineers poured into towns like worker ants. After great loss of life it was confirmed that neither bullets nor explosive charges had any effect on the creature. The theatre of this nightmare battle was their home and with that came new challenges. For how do you safely remove a cancer which is attached to everything you're trying to save? Special forces squads gathered intelligence regarding the behaviour of their adversary and regularly tested an array of weapon prototypes in the field. The highest register recorded was the Growth's annoyance and nothing more. Some of the bomb blasts even appeared to aid the creature's need to expand.

As the Growth spread, what remained of

The Growth

the government escaped by jets to France. They released a statement saying it was so they could better coordinate a strategy to save the remaining populous. Leaders spoke of finding answers in laboratories which was a bitter reminder of a mismanaged pandemic. Further fuel to the fires on the streets. Those who remained on home soil saw it for what it was, and the remaining thin veil of decency fell. Deep bitterness manifested in extreme violence and soon what was happening above ground was as dangerous as what happened below.

The same news channels which speculated what the Growth was and where it had come from suddenly stopped live broadcasts. In their place was a message to abandon built up areas and stay away from access points to water. The people packed up useless items and gridlocked the roads with their cars. Panic over water supplies spread like a sickness with deadly consequences. Bottled water was smuggled and hidden lest you wanted to be stabbed with a screwdriver for it. What was left of the military set up safe zones in rural areas, but they soon became theatres for violence as civilians grew impatient for decisive action. This faded when the military squads sent out to battle the Growth came back smaller and smaller each week until one day none returned at all. Large groups of civilians wandered back to towns in the search of supplies and loved ones, but their

The Growth

numbers were thinned by either the violent gangs that patrolled the streets or the creature lurking below them.

*

Jack's squad had been decimated. So ineffective were their guns against the Growth, it had become more prudent to focus on their secondary objective which was to rescue any civilians from Zone C. This particular zone was what remained of the small-town centre of St Helens, which had mainly been reduced to hills of rubble. The roads were fractured as though a terrible earthquake had struck. It was through one such crack which the Growth had dragged most of Jack's squad to their excruciating doom. The remaining civilians and soldiers had scattered in all directions but the agonised howls, which Jack had heard from the wall he'd jumped behind, told him most had been caught. Jack had crawled away as quietly as he could over broken glass and concrete until he'd been able to get to his feet and run.

Now, exhausted, Jack stood at the bottom of a hill which a discarded sign told him was North Road. He squinted at the collapsed church tower which had fallen across the width of the road and destroyed the houses opposite. Jack tried to visualise what it must have been like to be caught under a rain of bricks from God almighty Himself and shook his head glumly. His mood was spiralling, and his thoughts became more sombre with every step out of town. All his squad were dead, and he didn't want to think of what may have happened to his family back home. Jack wasn't the strongest or the smartest, and he certainly wasn't the fittest.

Why am I alive? he wondered.

"Stop it!" Jack shouted to the ruins.

He called on the last of his energy reserves and training and set about negotiating his way through the smashed church and up the hill so he could get out of the town centre. Jack didn't know where he was heading exactly but he knew the more built up the area the more likely another brush with the Growth would occur.

Bricks and slate gave way under Jack's boots as he climbed over the destruction blocking the road. Each time debris clattered and fell away, he froze and awaited the wrath of the Growth. Jack sat atop the pile of rubble and could see the steep road ahead. He was surprised to see half of the terraced houses which lined the road were still intact. There was a distant shout, but it quickly died away, so Jack shuffled down the slope with all the grace of a falling elephant. Once more he checked for any rumbles below his dusty boots before marching up the hill with a purpose. The stride was quickly corrected by anguish as he saw signs of human debris in and around the houses he'd seen. One house near the top of

The Growth

the hill had all of its windows smashed in and when Jack looked through one the sight took his breath away and filled his eyes with a haze of hot tears. Murdered families stripped naked and piled on top of each other stared out at him with the glazed eyes of the dead. It seemed the Growth was not the only monster at play in these parts. Jack turned away and continued to the crest of the hill. The light was fading, and he needed to find safe shelter quickly.

The view from the top of the hill showed the road ran parallel with a park where a large fire flickered between the dark shapes of tree trunks. Jack could hear the boisterous laughter and whooping from near the flames and thought of the slaughter he'd just uncovered. There was no way he could retrace his steps back to where his squad had been decimated so Jack decided to sneak through the treeline until he was clear of the park. He used the darkness as cover and sneaked looks from behind the larger trees. There were at least fifteen men around the fire, and it was clear to Jack from their behaviour they were under the influence of drugs. Most were bare-chested, some danced while others babbled at the sparks whenever more branches were thrown to the flames.

Jack moved around two more trees and felt his stomach flip as he noticed a charred leg protruding from the base of the fire. He needed to get out of the park quickly, but he

The Growth

also needed to be quiet. Thankfully, the men were so confident the Growth couldn't reach them in the park, their noise covered the sound of Jack crunching over twigs and leaves. There were two more trees available as cover which would take him twenty metres away from the group. If he stayed low, Jack was certain he could go unnoticed after the trees. He moved expertly to the first tree as something heavy was thrown on the fire to roars of approval. Jack dared not look back and instead walked quickly to the last tree. He stepped around it and collided with a man who had just finished urinating.

"Woah!" the man yelled through a gurning mouth.

Jack's eyes were as wide as the others were dilated but he still had the presence of mind to grab the man in a headlock to shut him up. He applied pressure to the man's throat who in turn clawed and scratched his wrist. A fiercely powerful beam from a torch landed on Jack and he immediately released his grip on the man and set off running.

"Over there!" a voice screamed. "Get him!"

The sound of running feet and panting breath seemed to be all around Jack and he sprinted away from the torchlight.

"He's going to the gate!"

Jack felt bile rising as he ran through the gate. His body wanted to give up, but he knew

The Growth

to do so meant death. No way was he going to be more fuel for the fire in the park. He ran past abandoned cars onto a housing estate and desperately looked for somewhere to hide but the gang of men were too close for him to stop and properly look. They thundered behind him, high on drugs, and howling threats like crazed animals. Jack banked right and saw a few ransacked shops. An abandoned bakery had been decorated with two bodies which had been bound to trolleys. A pack of dogs were worrying at something in the gutter but then scattered when the heavy footfall of the pursuit came their way. The street was returning to the main road Jack had followed up the hill, but it was too open for him to hide, and his stamina could not match the energy which the drugs had given those who chased him.

A corner shop came into view on his left and behind it was a high gate which protected an alleyway leading to the backs of rows of houses. Jack burst forward and threw himself at the gate before pulling himself up and over. As he looked back, he saw the group scrambling across the street to get to him. Jack jumped down, raced past bins, and discarded household items which lay in the alleyway. He heard the metal gate groan with the weight of his pursuers and looked desperately at the backs of the houses set either side of him. Jack needed to pick a house to hide in before he ran out of time and decided he'd vault over the wall

The Growth

into the next house he reached.

Mercifully, the rear door had been left wide open, evidence of someone leaving in a hurry. The severely damaged kitchen area showed why. The Growth had visited recently, and Jack slowed his movements in response.

"You check over there!"

Jack tip-toed further into the house in response to the shouting from the alleyway. He imagined the men splitting up to check each house and sure enough by the time he'd reached the staircase he heard steps in the kitchen.

"The doors open on this one," a gruff voice called out.

I'm fucked, Jack thought.

Then a plan came to him thanks to the clarity of mind only afforded to those about to make a last stand. A plan which would take the gang down with him and scrub out the stain which had blighted the area for longer than the Growth. Jack grabbed the object which had inspired him and ran up the stairs as noisily as possible.

"He's in here!" a voice from the kitchen called out.

Jack ran into what looked like a teenagers bedroom and grabbed a chair. He dragged it into the bathroom and switched on the battery powered radio he'd discovered downstairs. The sound of furniture breaking rumbled up the stairs as the gang occupied a space too

The Growth

small for their numbers. Jack wedged the chair under the door handle and thumbed the tuning dial on the radio. Static greeted him as men began to race up the stairs to him. The gang stomped into each room until absurd Calypso music began to play from the bathroom. Jack looked at the radio in disbelief. It was hard to believe life was carrying on as normal at a distant radio station somewhere out in the world.

"He's in there!"

There was a crash against the door which sounded as though one of the men had simply ran into it and then others began to bash at it violently.

"I want his boots," Jack heard one of them say.

With trembling hands he turned the volume up as loud as it would go and placed the radio onto the windowsill. The sunshine music bounced off every surface as Jack put his weight against his barricade. His plan had one main requirement. He needed the drugs to keep the men's inhibitions at bay so their idiotic voices and actions would continue to be as loud as they had been in the park. The door was beginning to give under their weight as the entire gang formed like a rugby scrum on the landing outside the bathroom.

Jack closed his eyes until he swore he felt the floor vibrating. He looked to see the pipework under the sink shake and smiled to

The Growth

the chaotic destruction which began to sound from the kitchen below. He waited until the bath was pulled through the floor by slimy tendrils and then removed the chair from under the broken door. The men rushed in as best they could and clawed and struck at him. Jack submitted and fell under the crush which jammed the gang in place. As the men on top of him began to shriek to the burns from the Growth's embrace, Jack smirked in defiance. Steel drums played him out from the world.

The Growth

This House Is a Tomb

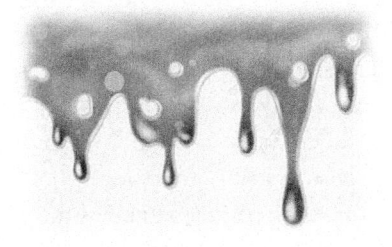

It was 2:30 a.m. when Tax pulled the blanket around him and shivered. The pipework below the street he'd always lived on were owned by the Growth now. It used them as a network to move freely as it searched out the noise and movement above. Sometimes it seemed like the monster had moved on but then it would give a reminder it was all around, as though no heating or water supply wasn't enough. Yesterday, there had been a large gas explosion which had shaken the house and caused Tax to flinch so hard he tweaked a muscle in his neck. He thought about it now and his jaw began to tremble as he sat on the sofa in the darkness. Tax told himself his teeth were chattering because he was cold rather than admit he was terrified. He gave a tell-tale look at the kitchen door he had barricaded shut and squeezed his eyes together until it hurt.

"I'm sorry," he whimpered softly.

By the time he had fought his way through the crowds to get home he had been met with a house lying in an odd silence compared to the

The Growth

carnage elsewhere in the street. The glimmer of hope he'd held tightly when searching his brother's home had been crushed when he saw the destruction in the kitchen. Cupboards were crushed and the oven was on its side while the sink had fallen into a large hole which had inexplicably arrived in the room. It looked as though the kitchen had been submerged in fluid for a short while before being drained. Tax felt like he was staring into a shipwreck rather than a room in the perfectly fine house he'd been in before he'd left to deal with Nicky Connor. The heart of the home was ruined, and his brother and niece had been replaced by two dark stains on what remained of the lino floor. Tax had told himself to block the entrance to the kitchen in an attempt to make the house safe again, but the real reason was he couldn't bear seeing those stains ever again. The bathroom had been as he'd left it, but he sealed that off too. A tomb for future explorers to ponder on perhaps.

Tax looked at the half empty bottle of water near his feet and tried to ignore his thirst. He tried to think of what had come for them at Nicky's place and what had swept away the last of his family but found only confusion and a frustrated sense he wasn't quite smart enough to find a solution.

Maybe if I figure it out, the bad things will stop happening.

The noise in his ears was getting worse

The Growth

again. Usually Tax would put his music on or maybe the television, but nothing was working in the house anymore. He needed to get out yet the compulsion to stay was a chained weight of loyalty around his neck.

The sounds of violence from in front of his house replaced the ringing in his ears and Tax looked to the front door. Of course there had been a constant stream of action over the past few days but something about the timing of this incident awakened a feeling within him. Tax rushed to the window and made a break in the blinds to peer through. A tall, skinny man with a backpack was being set on by two men and a woman who Tax recognised from the pub.

"Give it ere!" he heard the woman yell.

The skinny man displayed nothing but the wide eyes of paralysing fear.

"Last chance or I'll slash yer," the smallest man threatened.

Tax felt the cloud of grief and indecision dispersing from around his head. Here was something he knew how to do. Something at which he was good. Tax threw the door open and stepped out into the chilly morning. He was going to commit everything to helping people. His approach was immediately noticed.

"This has nowt do with you, Tax!" the bigger of the two men warned him.

The skinny man's head jerked from face to face at this new development, unsure of

The Growth

whether it made things better or worse.

"Leave him alone," Tax said coldly.

The group of three exchanged looks as though hoping they'd become telepathic overnight.

"Tax, we just want the bag, ok?"

The big man approached with his arms out in a gesture of calm and reassurance, but Tax watched his jaw clench and noticed the smaller man following a little too closely behind. Before a further word was uttered, Tax smashed his fist into the nearest man's throat. A gurgling sound acted as the soundtrack to the man's journey to his knees and Tax caught him savagely with a kick once he reached there.

"Bastard!"

The woman ran noisily away but Tax ignored her to fully concentrate on the man with the blade.

"You're fucking dead!"

Tax shook his head slowly and allowed the doubt to register in the man's mind. He watched it travel through the shaking knife and up the small man's arm. Once in his skull, the man sprinted after the woman in silence. The skinny man with the backpack was frozen in the middle on the road, staring with wide-eyed appreciation regarding the severity of the violence.

"Better get inside," Tax told him with a jab of his thumb to the open front door.

The Growth

The man followed on legs which were uncertain but too scared to change course.

<u>The Plan</u>

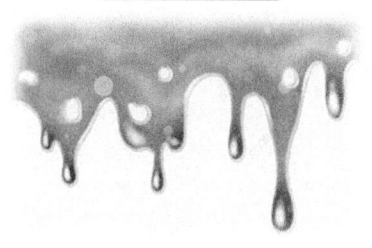

Kevin sat on his rucksack and tried to ignore the stench of urine clinging to the carpet below him. He pretended to clean his glasses on his jumper but was in actual fact trying to steal a look at the brute who had so far been his saviour. There was a roughness to the man on the sofa causing Kevin to feel uneasy. This was the type of person he might see on television or looking shady outside the train station. It was certainly not the kind of person Kevin had ever associated with before. The man took a small sip of his water and busied himself choosing what to pack into a gym bag. So far Kevin had only seen things that could be used to bludgeon someone to death making the cut. The way in which he had destroyed the man in the road was enough for Kevin to regard his saviour as dangerous and the very look of him oozed violence. Kevin eyed the large, scarred hands delving in and out of the gym bag and observed the strong physique which was currently being poorly concealed with a well-worn baggy t-shirt which proclaimed "Florida

The Growth

Paradise." It was a body which reminded it's observer of the cage fighters who seemed to be all the rage these days. There was plenty of muscle there but not like the steroid abusers which Kevin had seen plenty of. No, this was muscle built with a functional purpose. Kevin dared not think what that purpose was, although he could give an educated guess. There was a vulnerability to the man though, which Kevin had noticed once he'd been invited to sit down. The man's clear blue eyes didn't once make contact with his own and a general awkwardness seemed to overcome him reaching well beyond the meeting of two strangers. His shaved head also bore the shimmery paths of old scars and it twitched from side to side at the slightest noise which Kevin found a little irregular. The man had cauliflower ears but no broken nose. It seemed if the man saw the threat coming then things only went one way.

"Pretty, aren't I?"

Kevin twitched in horror at being caught out by the man who hadn't once appeared to notice he was being scrutinised.

"Why haven't you left?" Kevin asked in an attempt to shift direction away from his shame.

"Where would I go?"

Kevin immediately feels sorrow for the man. It was a sadness he knew the man wouldn't react kindly too, but he couldn't shake it.

The Growth

"The safe zones were on the news. Out of town."

"Tele's broke."

"You're going now though?" Kevin asks with a nod to the gym bag.

"I dunno. Just need to get out."

Tax gave a little look at the blockade in front of the kitchen door. Kevin followed the glance and had an inkling why the sorrow returned.

After an awkward silence, Kevin thinks of the cat and mouse nature of the past few days which culminated in his eventual brush with a knife wielding gang. Moving even small distances had become a dangerous hardship.

"Maybe we could help each other?"

"How?"

Kevin thought about the journal he'd moved from his bag to the seemingly more secure inside pocket of his coat and felt it there near his heart.

"I'm heading to a military base and as you can probably tell I could use somebody like you to get there."

"Like me?"

Kevin cursed himself for the misstep. It felt as though he had grown too confident around a wild animal and was about to suffer the sharp toothed consequence.

"Well, what I meant was the journey will probably be dangerous and as you saw I'm not the best at looking after myself."

The Growth

Now the man was speaking a language Tax could understand.

"So you need a bodyguard."

Kevin snorted at the title but on seeing the lack of returned amusement, swallowed his chuckle down.

"Yes, I suppose so."

"No."

"No?"

"That's what I said isn't it?"

Kevin nodded quickly and felt despair creep in at the prospect of travelling alone again.

"You can stay here but I'm going once it's light."

Kevin didn't really hear the statement and instead thought of the contents of the journal and the importance of his own mission.

"People out there need my help," the man on the sofa added as though to himself.

Kevin perked up and decided to change tact.

"We never introduced ourselves with all the excitement. I'm Kevin."

"Tax."

"Sorry?"

"Tax. People call me Tax."

"Tex."

"Tax!"

"Ok, erm Tax? What if I told you I'm trying to reach the army to tell them I have an idea of how to destroy this creature?"

The Growth

Tax looked directly at Kevin for the first time, who smiled nervously.

"So you would be helping every single person in this country," Kevin added.

Tax scratched his stubble and fidgeted with his ear. Much to Kevin's despair the man then returned to packing his gym bag.

"Does that sound like something you could help me with, Tax?"

The packing paused and a strange tension invaded the room causing the hairs on Kevin's arms to stand on end.

"You're not lying to me are yer?" Tax asked with an accusing point of a small axe.

Kevin waited until Tax had decided to pack the weapon before answering.

"No, no way. I've got an idea I think can stop this thing, but I need to get it to the army to make it happen."

"Is it a gun?"

"What? No."

"Bomb?"

"No, no it's a chemical formula."

Tax raised his eyebrows as though he'd just been told his next meal was something incredibly disappointing.

"Will it work?"

"Yes. I mean I hope so."

"Hope so?"

Tax measured the words as though trying to find weight in there meaning and whether it would buy his time.

The Growth

"I'm confident it will!" Kevin blurted out in desperation.

Even though confidence had been bleeding out of him ever since he'd left behind his house of failures, he couldn't afford to lose Taxs' help. Again there was much scratching of stubble and fiddling of ears.

"Ok."

"You'll come with me?"

"Yeah, get some sleep."

Kevin grinned like an idiot before closing his mouth to the stench of urine.

Bronze Medal

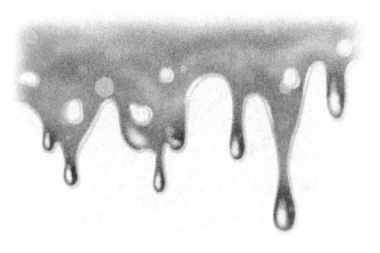

Emma sat under the clothes display with her knees drawn to her chest. The uncomfortable position was bracing her from the early hours of a new day but most of all it was keeping her legs out of view of the two men who even now called for her.

"Come on love, we just want to look in that bag of yours."

There was a small gap between dresses affording Emma a look at a wall mounted mirror. It was the first time she'd allowed herself to steal more than a glance at her own reflection and it did nothing to lift her spirits. Hair grown longer than she'd usually allow due to the natural volume of it and a puffy face which told the world there were no tears left. Emma self-consciously touched the years old bump in her nose from the break which hadn't been set properly. A set of legs wearing jeans and boots obscured her view.

"You don't need to hide; we won't hurt you."

Emma felt the crack of a smirk on the

mask she wore these days.

They think I'm hiding. This is a trap, dickheads.

In a movement only the well trained could perform with such fluidity, Emma rose through the gap while throwing a right uppercut. The brief feeling of the man's stubble on her knuckles sickened her but the thump of his unconscious skull on the shop floor did not. Emma swivelled to see the other man staring wide-eyed in the gloom. He was dressed all in black with a woolly hat on. Emma figured he was probably already a thief before all the shit had happened. He hesitated near the forced open shutters. Emma retrieved her rucksack from near her feet and held it aloft as though it were some artefact worth displaying.

"Come on then," she goaded.

The man's eyes darted from the bag to Emma, and then to his friend's skull which was now leaking.

"Mad cow!"

It was nothing more than a bleat of defiance before the thief rolled under the shutters and away. Emma glanced at the man laid out at her feet as though regarding a stain upon a carpet.

She hefted the bag over one shoulder and the plastic bottles within glugged in an almost enthusiastic manner. Emma thought of the worn photograph that lay in there too. A photograph so precious she'd had the peace of mind to place it in a food bag to prevent

The Growth

moisture spoiling it. Jane with a face slightly reddened by cocktails and the relentless Greek sunshine. In the picture she is pretending to sing into a miniscule, neon, plastic microphone which had arrived in her last glass. Emma smiled sadly and closed her eyes to trap a tear or two. For a moment she slowed her breathing and could almost hear Jane's infectious laughter.

Their last phone call had reached Emma from the busy office block where Jane had been making a name for herself in the media field. There were hurried exchanges of love and affection before the destruction and screams nearby the caller had muffled and then terminated the call. Emma refused to dwell on how the call ended. Refused to give up. There had to be some sign of her beloved at the office. Maybe Jane was still hiding there but with no means of making contact. Emma rushed under the shutters as though dragged by a new gravitational pull.

Operation Predator

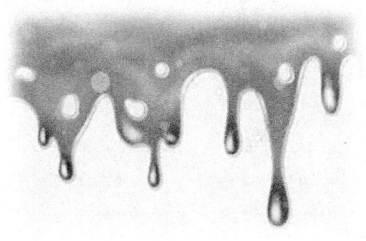

Section Alpha had been hastily thrown together and dropped on the outskirts of the city centre. All eight soldiers were a third of what remained of the 1st Intelligence, Surveillance and Reconnaissance Brigade. Like the majority of the 3rd Division, the 6th Division had been decimated in the early days of assuming the Growth could be met head on with perceived "superior" firepower. The ISR had been horrifically caught up in these massacres and so its surviving soldiers had been keen to volunteer after Brigadier Thomas' latest briefing. After bullets and shells had been found wanting it had fallen on the science branch to explore chemical solutions. The restraint usually reserved for such activities had been negated by the staggering death toll of millions. There was little point in regarding the danger to the general public when their numbers were already dwindling. All that mattered now was the annihilation of the Growth which threatened to reduce the UK to a deserted island.

The Growth

Section Alpha's objective was to test a potent nerve gas, nicknamed "Rattus 11" their science wing was extremely excited about. Special canisters had been fitted so they could be thrown by the soldiers once contact with the Growth was made. Once results had been "adequately observed" Section Alpha could call in Section Bravo, made up of the 16 Air Assault Brigade, for extraction via helicopter.

Wilson peered down his scope at the vast water treatment works and held his breath. Aerial reconnaissance had picked out the site to test the gas for a number of reasons. Primarily they knew for sure that the Growth's presence would be there, and that the surrounding woodland would aid Section Alpha's escape. The field directly after the tree's was perfect for a helicopter pick up and was far enough from the Growth given its current projected proportions. Section Alpha were also cynical enough to understand the theatre was far enough from base so the Growth wouldn't follow them "home."

"Corporal, why don't they just drop the cannisters out of the bloody helicopter?"

Wilson looked away from the scope into the camouflage painted face of Briers. A square-jawed Bristolian who's impatience couldn't be concealed by the woodland colours he wore.

"I dunno? Wind maybe?"

Briers scrunched his face and looked

around as though gauging the weather conditions with expert precision.

"You mean why have a dog and bark yourself?"

Wilson returned to the scope and smirked. "Yes."

"Gas Masks would have been nice, Corporal."

"A hot bath and pizza would be nice, but we don't have them either."

Briers chuckled before nervously stroking one of his gas canisters.

There was a momentary glare in the opposite treeline and Wilson tutted.

"Watch your scopes boys," he told the other fire team who prowled out of hearing range.

Wilson turned to regard the three men under his command. Picton and Williams crouched next to Briers.

"We keep low, and we move to the left flank quietly."

The three men nodded grimly.

"Quietly," Corporal Wilson reiterated for Briers' benefit.

The men moved off with nothing more than the rustle of grass and equipment. Wilson looked to the trees on the right but was satisfied to see the other team was out of sight. The water works had contained eight separate buildings but three had been destroyed by the probing movements of the Growth. Even so,

The Growth

the area was much bigger than Wilson had expected it to be when his team had first viewed the aerial reconnaissance photographs. The other team would be covered by trees right up until the point of contact whereas Wilson and his men would have to use one of the remaining buildings as cover to get close enough. Directly to the northern edge of the complex was a wide river which the Growth now occupied.

Wilson thought about how the early reports had the size of the creature being the size of a bus. When his battalion had first suffered heavy losses, the Growth had taken over the underground area of a single town which it was roughly the size of. Now it was present in most areas of the country, stretching through pipework from sewers to rivers and back again. The more it consumed the more it grew, a constant threat below the surface. Europe was watching nervously as they prayed the Growth wouldn't spill out into the North sea. For now the Growth seemed content to absorb the large island. The Prime Minister, hidden away, blocked any attempt for intervention by posturing and spinning a rhetoric of outdated nationalism. One of the best military machines in the world did not need "outside interference" and certainly the threat of nuclear escalation from abroad was not being taken lightly.

"Arsehole," Wilson muttered as they

reached the first building.

As boots on the ground, he would have certainly welcomed help from NATO allies. Briers peered around the side of the building and returned a nod for Wilson's benefit. The Corporal joined the man and saw their destination. Four concrete circles lay in a row. They were the size of small swimming pools with patchy grass surrounding them. Wilson noticed the wreaked observation decks strewn nearby. Further proof of the Growth's presence. Of course, they could simply walk to the banks of the river and toss the gas canisters in but the reach of the beast there would be too great for anyone to escape. The Growth was using the water treatment facility as one of its many junction points to access nearby towns and so the small pools the men stared at presented the best opportunity for a hit-and-run objective. Each member of the two teams carried a P2022 pistol only, rather than their usual assault weaponry to enable quicker movement. The decision had been made based on the Growth's complete resistance to conventional weapons and the only reason the teams weren't totally unarmed was due to the increasingly volatile actions of the ever-decreasing general public.

Corporal Wilson gestured for his team to move off, so they stayed low and skirted the building until there was no choice but to break cover and stride out onto the grass. The second team moved with the same purpose from the opposite side of the inspection pools, a perfect mirror image of Wilson and his men. There was an occasional swishing sound from the water.

It's in there and we're bloody running towards it.

With this unnerving clarity, Wilson almost ordered the teams to abort but they were already in position around the pools. Reluctantly he looked across to the other fire team, nodded, and pulled out his pistol. James who stood opposite Wilson was the only other soldier to draw his gun as all others waited to prime their gas canisters. Both men fired two shots into the air and the effect on the water was immediate as frantic ripples soon revealed the oily mass reaching out in all directions to find the source of the noise. Wilson holstered his pistol quickly and twisted the top on the canister like they'd been shown. As he was throwing it towards the mass his horrified eyes took in the moment James was lanced through the chest. Noxious green gas left a trail in the air, but it wasn't thick enough to cover the sight of James writhing in agony like a worm on a fishing hook. Wilson heard yelling all around, yet he was transfixed on the man opposite who briefly held his hands out for help. Then he was gone. Thrown forty feet into the air as though he weighed nothing more than a tennis ball. The body returned to the ground with a sickening thud which broke it and snapped

The Growth

Wilson back to reality. All canisters had been thrown and the remaining members of James' team were sprinting away with understandable cowardice.

"Corporal!" Briers screamed.

"Go! I need to see."

Briers hesitated, caught in two minds of what to do. Picton and Williams had no such issue and quickly barrelled past Wilson as they headed for the evac zone. The green smoke filled two of the pools and was billowing up like signal smoke. Wilson and Briers took a few steps backwards as the thrashing from the pool intensified.

Come on, come on.

Large splashes came from the surface of the water and then half a dozen arms of the growth emerged only ten feet away from the two men. Wilson instinctively reached for his gun before realising it was a futile action. Briers took a step forward and threw his second canister onto the ground near the tentacles. The gas washed over the scene as Wilson continued to back off.

"Get out of there, Briers!"

The branches of the Growth suddenly stood erect in an obscene gesture. They writhed wildly and then disappeared back under the water and out of sight. Briers turned to Wilson and punched the air in delight. He grinned at the success of the gas and was in the process of yelling about it to the Corporal

The Growth

when the wind changed. Wilson watched as the green smoke washed across Briers' face and the man briefly vanished from view.

"Briers?"

There was silence from both the cloud of gas and the water behind it.

"Briers!"

Wilson took a step backwards just as Briers sprinted out of the gas and violently collided with him.

"What the hell's the matter with you?" Wilson cursed as he tried to get back to his feet.

Before he had completed the task, Briers was on him. Wilson caught a glimpse of the man's face which wore an unnatural expression of rage and glee combined. Then the punches began to rain down on him.

"Briers, stop it man!"

Wilson wriggled underneath his attacker so that most of the blows were glancing shots. Yet Briers' energy wasn't faltering and if anything, the punches were getting harder with murderous intent. A blow connected with Wilson's face and a chilling pain surrounded his left eye. He was shocked and angered to know his cheekbone was fractured then the next strike loosened some of his teeth. Wilson began to dig his fingers into Briers' face and used his free leg to deliver a knee to the man's groin. Briers howled in a way that brought shivers to Wilson's flesh but still he managed to throw the man off balance so he could get

The Growth

to his feet. Briers jumped up and snarled, his lips gurning uncontrollably. Wilson had his pistol trained at the man's chest.

"Don't," he warned through his bloodied mouth.

Briers leapt forward and Wilson squeezed the trigger twice. Both men ended up in a heap but this time one of them was lifeless.

Wilson wept as he squirmed from under the dead man. His face was in agony as he watched the green gas dissipate. He needed to hurry back through the woods before the helicopter left without him. The water was completely still so at least the mission had been a success. As Wilson staggered past trees, he already knew he would omit his fight with Briers from the report.

*

<u>Mission Report Corporal Wilson 04/05/22.</u>

Section Alpha moved from the drop zone to the target.

As planned, Alpha split into two fire teams to encircle the target.
Both teams deployed their canisters of Rattus 11 effectively, but Lance Corporal James was KIA by the Growth.

Lance Corporal James' team panicked and retreated to the evac zone as did two members of my own

The Growth

(Privates Picton and Williams). For the record they had effectively deployed their canisters prior to their tactical retreat.

I stayed to observe the effectiveness of Rattus 11 alongside Private Briers.

Private Briers was KIA by the Growth before the Rattus 11 forced it to retreat.

I returned to the evac zone to rendezvous with Section Bravo for a successful extraction back to base.

Notes from Brigadier Thomas.

Let the records show that I am recommending Corporal Wilson for promotion. It is clear he displayed the valour and heroism which has been the mainstay of the British army throughout history.

Due to the reaction Rattus 11 gas had on the Growth, and the acceptable level of casualties, Operation Predator can be declared a success, and it is advised that we move forward in preparation for Operation Breakout immediately.

The Bodyguard

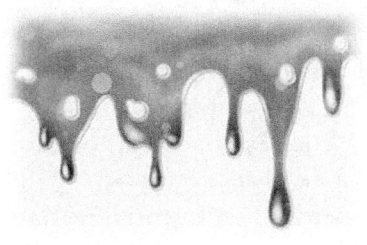

Survivors had become shuffling packs of refugees. Shorn from their personal kingdoms they were desperately afraid as they tried to escape a horror beyond their control. Kevin eyed one such group as they walked along a road cluttered with abandoned vehicles and couldn't help but smirk.

"What yer smiling for?"

Tax's voice had an accusing tone as though his walking partner had laughed at a funeral service.

"Nothing I-. I was just thinking that the further along we get, the more people are looking like groups of refugees."

"That's funny to you?"

"Not at all no," Kevin blushed. "I was wondering how many of these have sneered at people fleeing war zones in Syria. How many turned their backs on other human beings drowning in the North Sea. Even now they probably can't connect the dots."

Tax looked across to the grass slope where families rested. Battered suitcases at their feet

The Growth

full of useless belongings.

"That's the people we're trying to help, isn't it?"

Kevin emptied his lungs with a tired sigh.

"Yes. Yes, I suppose it is."

Tax gave Kevin a quick look of mistrust from over his shoulder and stepped carefully around a patch of oil from a nearby crash. The man would look menacing while picking flowers and Kevin was glad of it. So far, they had been left alone by the other wretched travellers and he put this down to the intimidating aura Tax constantly emitted. They had of course avoided built-up areas wherever possible, but the next town was too big to go around without costing them time from a clock which was already running at double-speed.

Tax stood in the middle of the road on the outskirts of the town and stared at the few high-rise buildings growing from the industrial ruin. Kevin thought of how the man looked like a boxer psyching himself up before going into battle against a much larger opponent. In a way he supposed he was.

"Are you bothering?"

Kevin nodded and wondered at the copious amounts of black smoke the town was belching out.

"Looks like most of the place burned."

"Came here years ago on a stag do," Tax nodded at the town. "Full of idiots."

Kevin thought of the man on a night out

The Growth

and smirked. Once more Tax caught him.

"Bit of a weirdo aren't you."

Kevin instinctively wanted to disagree but after a brief internal highlight reel of his life, conceded the point.

The sound of a scooter engine reached them before they saw the shirtless rider weaving expertly around piles of debris. Both men stopped walking to watch as the scooter slowed to a halt at the end of the road they were travelling down. The small engine hiccupped as the rider looked left and right to choose the best road into town. Kevin felt as though he was watching a silent movie as the scooter sets off on the road leading left. An abandoned van hid the exposed manhole so neither the men nor the rider could see the Growth lying in wait. A black lance smashed into the wheels which sent the rider flying through the air like a crash test dummy. The impact was deadly, and Kevin turned away with a wince. However, his eyes betrayed his wishes and returned him to the scene to watch the broken body get dragged helplessly towards consumption.

"We'll go right," Tax said almost cheerfully.

*

Emma crouched in the scorched remains of a small shop that afforded her minimal cover

The Growth

from the large group of violent looking men and women. Her eyes watered and she coughed as quietly as possible into her sleeve. The group was scavenging together, and Emma hoped the obvious destruction she was hiding in would deter anyone from getting too close. Windows were smashed, laughter rang out, and Emma nervously glanced along the road for any points which the Growth could emerge from. The inside of the shop opposite had turned up some booze and the group hooted like chimps. A short man took too much of a swig for the others' liking and is soon thrown to the ground and kicked severely by multiple sets of dirty boots.

Animals.

Emma almost hopes they come for her now but knows she'll never make it to Jane if she takes on every mob between here and the office block.

"Go and check over there," one of the men shouts.

Emma cringes at the hand pointing towards her hiding place.

"Piss off, it's all burnt!"

Emma can't see the complainer, but she prays his point of view is considered.

"Do you want a smack? Get in there!"

There's a sudden cacophony of noise which causes Emma to flinch back, as her mind is sure she's being attacked. Screams come from the road, or where the road used to be. A

The Growth

thick cloud of dust obscures the view and Emma can't see the shops opposite her hiding place. The cries turn into yelps of agony below the spectral cloud of debris before an eventual breeze partially lift it away allowing Emma a glimpse of the twisted carnage. An area of around twenty-five metres in length, and covering the width of the road, has completely sunken in. Emma stepped as near to the edge as she dared to bear witness to the violent end of the gang who would have done her great harm only moments earlier. The man who had pointed her way was now attempting to drag his broken legs over crushed pipework while his tortured cries follow the dust cloud to the heavens. Emma looked away from the man who's hyperventilating journey was a sickening display of courage over sense. The Growth already filled half of the crater which it shared with clumps of concrete and ever diminishing body parts. Part of it came forward like a snail's upper tentacle, but instead of an eye at the end there was a hooked shape which dragged the last woman backwards. She locked eyes with Emma, yet her mouth couldn't address the burning agony that quickly overcame her as the consumption concluded. The Growth filled three quarters of the pit now and the man huffed with his back to the earth.

"Help me!"

There was nothing around to lower into the pit and Emma doubted the man would

The Growth

have the strength left to pull himself out in time. What concerned Emma more was she wasn't entirely sure she would help the man even if it were a possibility. The man's larynx broke new ground with the harrowing tone of his screams as the searing grasp of the Growth pulled at his broken legs. Emma turned from the crater and moved away as quietly as possible before the creature bubbling below could reach out to her. Once around the corner of the street, Emma's body began to quake with despairing sobs which only ceased when dry heaving from her empty stomach took over.

*

    The signs of battle lay strewn in the streets Kevin and Tax stalked down. Scorch marks scarred the roads, glass appeared to have fallen like rain, and abandoned military vehicles blocked most junctions. Even Tax had become more careful in his movements and Kevin was no longer in danger of falling behind. The taller buildings appeared to lean over the men who self-consciously kept looking to the windows above as though expecting someone to be spying on them. So far there had been no sign of life, only the stains of death. Tax turned to say something but was interrupted by scurrying feet up ahead. A woman and a young boy scrambled into view and immediately froze in

The Growth

fear at seeing the two men.

"It's ok," Tax said in a soft voice that surprised Kevin.

The boy of around ten years old moved a step closer to the woman who slowly held a knife up towards the men. Kevin felt as though the blade had pierced his heart as the sorrow of the situation briefly overcame him. What had happened to the pair to make them seemingly feral?

"No, it's ok."

In a blink of an eye they were gone, a scampering of feet from around the corner and nothing more. Tax turned to Kevin wearing the defeat like a newly acquired outfit.

"What are we gonna do, mate?"

A brick bounced off the nearest ruined car before Kevin had a chance to answer. The men quickly shrunk back yet Tax was struck in the shoulder and back with stones which sent him clattering to the broken road. Kevin rushed to help him up but was painfully scragged backwards by his hood. The man holding it swiftly crumpled him with a barrage of punches to his stomach and ribs. Kevin fell to his knees and remained there like a puppet as the grip on his hood remained. Tax lay unmoving on the road as more footsteps, presumably belonging to the stone throwers, scurried to Kevin. Fear rose up like bile and he blinked tears away from his eyes so he could stare at his prone bodyguard.

The Growth

Get up! Come on, Tax, please!

Two men walked in front of Kevin and obscured his view. They wore layers of clothing like poor people's armour and sneered down at him, but Kevin refused to look past the cricket bats they clutched.

"Go and check on him," the voice of Kevin's captor said.

"Who made you boss, Dave?"

"Don't use my name, *Alan*!"

Alan postured and Kevin felt the grip on him relax a little as Dave prepared to fight the man. The third, yet to be named and shamed, man shuffled uncomfortably.

"Come on lads, let's not do this now eh?"

Kevin looked at Alan just as a fist wrapped around from behind him. The force of the blow was horrific, and Kevin winced as the man's jaw was knocked completely from its hinge before the owner fell with a sickening thud.

"Bastards!" Tax roared as he swung murderous punches towards shocked face.

Kevin was awestruck at the primal rage Tax was unleashing. It made his hair stand on end and he felt his own jaw clench in satisfaction as though rooting for a particular gladiator of old. The previously unseen man gurgled as his nose was caved in. Kevin heard the sound of wood on tarmac as the cricket bat was dropped and he heard the click of Dave's flick knife being opened behind him. The man

The Growth

took a step towards Tax, so Kevin instinctively grabbed at the nearest jean clad leg in a lame act of defiance. Dave looked down as though he'd stepped in dog shit and raised the knife. Kevin looked up in terror and was summoning pleas when the cricket bat struck Dave's temple with a death strike. The sound was as though a thousand champagne corks had been popped in unison and the man's eyes immediately rolled back. A new hand pulled at him now and Kevin twitched in fear. Tax pulled him upright, still huffing from the exertion of the fight.

"You alright?"

Kevin nodded rapidly and felt faint from the adrenaline bleeding out of him in buckets.

"Brave but stupid," Tax scorned his actions.

Kevin smiled weakly and half shrugged.

"You're the brains and I'm the brawn, ok?"

"Yeah, I know," Kevin said meekly.

"I'm the looks too," Tax announced with a mischievous smirk as he gathered the other cricket bat.

Kevin's smile quickly disappeared when Tax offered him the bloodstained bat.

"Can I have the clean one?"

Tax rolled his eyes as though he were reluctantly having to tolerate the demands of a princess.

"Ok. Let's check their pockets and get out of here."

The Growth

The Brotherhood of Change and Growth

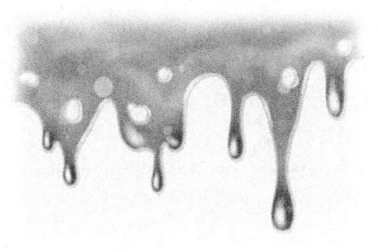

The Growth had been the best thing to happen to Michael Applewood. He had lost absolutely everything the week before the cleansing burn from the underground had begun. His software business had lost out on the only contract big enough to save it from going under and when he had numbly returned home, he had caught his wife in bed with his neighbour. Michael had ascended the ladders to his loft conversion and refused to come down. At first, he had wanted to die and then he came around to the idea of wanting his wife, neighbour, and colleagues to die. After days of plotting and fantasising, Michael emerged from his musky lair only to be met with the screams of many.

It had seemed like the whole street was singing from the same hymn sheet. A terrible song of agony and sorrow appalling to anyone nearby but to Michael Applewood it sounded like a chant of rebirth and new beginnings. His

The Growth

wretched wife had begged him to lower the ladders so she could escape the landing. Michael was somewhere close to arousal when the strange substance washed over her in a show of fire and brimstone. Her smug face turned to glue right there under his spying position. Michael had cried and begged in the small hours above his wife's sleeping head and now God had answered his prayers. He had watched in awe as this substance of justice moved from his landing and back towards the bathroom until it was out of sight.

Michael had emerged from the loft as a new man. Albeit one dressed in pyjamas. Michael's dressing gown had been draped over the banister that skirted the landing and as he had been putting it on, he had noticed the hood had been brushed by his saviour. A white, burnt stain on the black fabric which confirmed to Michael he had been chosen. He had proudly pulled the hood over his head and walked out of his old life to spread the word of his new one.

Now, Michael stood at the altar of his church. The building had once been a car rental showroom and the altar was actually a receptionist's desk. Yet nothing could discourage Michael as he passionately addressed the thirteen other members of The Brotherhood of Change and Growth.

"Brothers, let us take a moment to consider the great adversity that we have

The Growth

overcome to be here today."

Michael gave a theatrical wave of his hand from behind the desk and the thirteen men nodded and smiled warmly back at him.

"You are all survivors because the Growth deemed you worthy to walk these lands long after the sinners have been consumed. Each one of you lived because you were chosen by God to aid Him with the great reset."

Michael thought of the threats and the beatings he'd endured since venturing out to preach and found his throat contort with emotion.

"It has not been easy to find you, my brothers. No, it hasn't been easy but what trial of righteousness ever is?"

More smiles and impassioned nodding greeted Michael's words as he reached under the desk and produced a small tin of white gloss paint.

"As you know, the Growth not only touched my heart and soul, but it showed me the way by leaving its mark on my earthly garment."

Michael walked around the desk and bowed his head so the men could appreciate the white smudge on his hood.

"Now let us begin," he smiled at them and retrieved a paintbrush from his pocket.

Each man wore a jacket, coat, or sweater with a hood, and they pulled them up over their heads. Michael observed the line of men with

The Growth

tears in his eyes. The ruinous past that had rejected him had been washed away to reveal a paradise where anything was possible.

"We have watched from the shadows as He took so many sinners from these streets. The wretched built their towns and cities upon his glory and so for now there is only so much He can do from underground. It is on us, my brothers, to help round up the remaining unworthy and feed them to this gift which has been displayed to us."

The men murmured in delight and danced on the spot in jubilation. Michael noticed brother Darren standing still with his head bowed but continued, nonetheless.

"So as I anoint you all as my disciples, I ask you to chant the words that show Him the unity which will be unbroken in these final days before the great reset.

"Atop and below. Atop and below. Atop and below," the men cried in unison.

Michael walked down the line and with one stroke painted a white patch on each hood.

"We change for the Growth," he sighed to each man.

"Atop and below. Atop and below."

Michael came to brother Darren who wasn't chanting. Instead the man clenched his jaw and stared at his shoes.

"Is there something you would like to say, brother Darren?"

The other men stopped chanting and

The Growth

turned their heads towards the man. Michael felt hot coals in his belly at the thought the ceremony was in jeopardy of being sabotaged. Brother Darren looked up at him with eyes which seemed to shake with anger.

"I can't do this anymore!"

"Do *what?*" Michael hissed, his tone full of warning.

"This!"

Brother Darren removed his hood and held his arms out to the room.

"All this bullshit," he spat. "It was worth putting up with when it meant staying safe and sharing supplies but this, this is too much."

Michael Applewood saw he was no longer speaking with Brother Darren. No, it was simply Darren who stood before him now. He gave a look left and then right and Darren was immediately seized by those nearest to him.

"Let go of me!"

Michael placed the tin of paint at his feet and carefully rested the brush on the rim. He pulled the artist's scalpel from the deep pocket of his robe and removed the plastic guard.

"Silence," he warned Darren.

The much larger frames of Brother Gary and Brother Mark held Darren as Michael addressed the room.

"How wise is the Growth to present one final test of our faith? How fitting is it I should be supported by twelve disciples and not thirteen?"

The Growth

With that, Michael swept the blade across Darren's throat. He was caught off guard by the high-pressure stream of blood which sprayed his face. The warm salty liquid was the final insult Darren would hurl at the Brotherhood of Change and Growth as he sagged to his knees.

"Let him go," Michael told Brother Gary and Brother Mark.

Darren's face hit the tiles with a crack as Michael returned the scalpel to his pocket.

"Atop and below. Atop and below," the chanting resumed.

Michael wiped blood from his eyes and smiled affectionately at his twelve disciples.

"We will take him to the pit as our first offering to our righteous father."

Michael picked up the paint pot and continued down the line.

Birthday Shoes

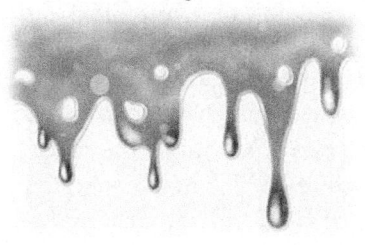

Emma stood across the road from the office block where Jane spent thirty-seven hours a week when a sudden pang of anxiety caused her to grab a nearby lamp post to steel herself against the nauseating giddiness. The building was a concrete slap to the face of her dwindling hopes. Its bottom floors had been consumed by fire and the glass had been shed like fur from a cat. Emma found she was numbly crossing the road to get closer, the crunch of shards under her boots pulling her from her trance.

If she stayed, then she's dead.

Emma looked at the ruins of a fancy reception area, past the lifts to where she knew the stairwell to be. Thankfully, the tons of fallen debris have not blocked the path to the higher floors. The seventh floor, second office on the left where she dreamed her beloved would be waiting with open arms and tear-soaked kisses.

"I wouldn't if I were you."

Emma turned to her left quickly to see a

man in his fifties propped up against an upturned taxi. His face was covered in ash, and he wore a business suit ripped in several places, so it flapped about like an old flag. Emma's reflex instinct was to warn the man to keep away but then she noticed the crimson puddle he was sitting in. The man coughed blood into the back of his hand and gestured at the large sliver of metal fusing him with the underside of the car.

"Explosion." the man stated with a nod towards the destroyed reception. "When I woke up, I was stuck like this and by the time my ears had stopped ringing, the screams had stopped too."

Emma would have vomited if she had had anything left to give to the task. She looked over her shoulder hopelessly.

"There's nothing in there for you," the pale faced man told her.

Emma took a step towards him, suddenly enraged at the gall of the man to tell her what she already felt in her heart.

"She's in there!"

The man looked down at the metal holding him together. Emma's anger dissipated.

"I'll come back, ok?" was all she could think to say.

"Why?" was the response as Emma made her way into the broken reception area.

The climb was more than she'd expected

The Growth

but nothing was going to stop her from hurdling, jumping, and squeezing her way upwards. Between the sounds of her own labours she could hear the building groan and sigh as though it were in pain. By the time Emma was on the seventh floor the angle of the floor was that of a ship battling a storm ridden sea.

"Jane?"

Her voice sounded dry and unnatural while the words clung in her throat with threats to choke her. The silence returned was heavy and bleak. Emma looked at the corporate corridor leading to Jane's office. Every surface was discoloured and stained as though the building had been dunked under water before being left to dry under a frigid winter sun. Emma pushed thoughts of the Growth from her mind, yet she still stumbled over her own feet as she reached the closed office door.

Is that my hand? Emma thought as she reached for the handle.

The sense of a bad dream threatened to suffocate as the interior of Jane's office was revealed to Emma's tearful eyes. No glass remained within the large window frame and the blinds noisily flapped between the interior and exterior. Emma scanned over the broken office furniture to the coat stand which had been used to smash the window through. A fallen filing cabinet in the corner gave Emma a last glimmer of hope but Janet wasn't hiding

The Growth

behind it. As she stood near the window, she saw a sight that broke the remaining pieces of her soul. On the ledge was one of Janet's expensive designer shoes. A birthday treat for sealing promotion. Emma dropped down noisily onto the side of the filing cabinet like she'd been switched off. She knew if she looked out of the window, to the parking area behind the office block she would see her broken angel. The injured man out front heard Emma's howl and closed his eyes to the sorrow of it before breathing his last breath.

Time had continued to move on, but Emma was left behind, frozen in the moment of her failure.

I should have been here.

Emma thought of what she could have done and quickly concluded she would simply have stood on the ledge alongside Janet. She imagined holding hands as the ground whistled towards them. Anything was better than the hurt in her stomach and chest she now endured.

Do it, coward.

The blinds slapped the window frame once more and Emma looked at the clouds passing by. She heaved herself to a standing position and wrestled with heartbreak and her coaches' teaching of not quitting.

"Sorry," she said to all the people in her head and took a step towards the window.

A terrible creak squealed from near the

The Growth

open door and Emma felt the floor move beneath her feet. She tried to grab the window frame, missed, and then fell through to the sixth floor. Emma scrunched her eyes shut and braced yet the wind was taken from her as she bounced off the fallen divider of the toilet stall. The wood snapped and bounced Emma onto a large sink which broke under her weight. Emma felt the top of her right arm which was wet from the gash which the ceramic had put there. A clattering in the corridor outside told her she wasn't alone and soon enough there was a strange shadow on the floor tiles beyond the destroyed door.

Emma looked around for escape but the destruction in the ceiling was out of reach and the room contained no windows. A wet slap turned her head back to the door in time to see a leg-sized portion of the Growth dragging along the floor. Emma's eyes grew wide as more and more of the creature came into view. Soon the door frame was buckling under the mass filling the corridor outside. The rhythmic pulse of excitement the mass displayed disgusted Emma, but she couldn't tear herself away from the sight. At times, the Growth was black and shiny like oil and then it would appear to be translucent so Emma could see through it to the wall behind. The Growth showed her human ribcages and skulls as it poured slowly into the bathroom. Porcelain shattered and Emma saw snake-sized parts of

The Growth

the thing rising up from the broken toilets. Another tendril appeared through the pipe shorn from the sink Emma had fallen on. It was hard to comprehend the Growth had been beneath her feet every mile of her journey and yet here it was. The vastness was staggering, and Emma felt the hollow effects of defeat as she backed away as far as the room would allow.

No wonder you jumped, my love, she thought.

The Growth was wreaking the ceiling as it moved towards her and it's arms, if that's what you could call something that numbered thousands, were only a metre away from her now. A massive bang interrupted the sizzling progression of the creature as an explosion rocked the sixth floor. Emma braced expecting another fall but the wall nearest the sinks collapsed in on itself instead. A soldier appeared in the room's new exit.

"Come on!" he yelled.

Emma hurdled debris and nearly collided with the man who practically dragged her out into the corridor before heading for the stairwell.

"We've got to hurry," he called over his shoulder. "That was my only grenade!"

"Shoot it then!"

They were clattering down the stairs before the soldier answered.

"Shooting does fuck all!"

He turned to give Emma a stern look to show

The Growth

the lesson had been learned the hard way and then he continued the dizzying descent to the blackened reception area. Emma could hear pandemonium following close behind as the Growth poured itself after them. For a moment she simply stopped and waited.

If bullets and grenades can't stop it, then what's the point?

The soldier was nearly out of sight and Emma shook herself from her slump, choosing survival over despair again.

Once outside, the pair retreated to their haunches in an attempt to breathe freely again.

"Guns just get its attention, that's all."

The soldier held up his L119A1 carbine as though he were showing Emma a major source of shame and embarrassment. Emma ignored the weapon and was instead struck with how youthful the soldier looked. He must have been no more than nineteen years of age.

"Let's go and check on him."

Emma followed the soldier's nod to the injured businessman who had warned her earlier. The man's head appeared to be slumped unnaturally to the side and Emma knew he'd gone even though she continued to walk to him. There was a clang of metal from behind and then the soldier roared in agony. A tendril stretched out from a storm drain and was wrapped around the soldier's ankle. Emma could see smoke coming off the material which was fusing with the man's flesh. The young

The Growth

soldier ignored his earlier advice and shot at his attacker. Emma saw that any bullet which didn't ricochet away was simply absorbed by the Growth.

"Help me!"

Emma grabbed the soldier's outstretched hand and gagged on the stench of burning flesh. As she pulled on the man's hand, he released a pitiful sob. Emma looked down to see his leg had been torn off from below his knee. The Growth held a booted stump with flesh being burned away like fat on a griddle pan.

"Come on, come on!" Emma hissed as she half-dragged the soldier towards the fallen businessman.

By the time the pair had reached the crashed taxi, the soldier's face was as white as the dead man who was pinned to the vehicle. Mercifully, the Growth retreated back into the drainage system, seemingly reaching its limits for now. Emma quickly took her belt off as the soldier convulsed violently on the ground. After several botched attempts she managed to create a tourniquet, but the charred stump was still spurting arterial blood at an alarming rate.

"Please, please." the soldier begged.

Emma turned her attention to the dying man's emotional needs and held his hands and made sure he could see her face. She smiled for him through tears.

"What's your name, mate?" Emma asked.

The Growth

The grip on her hand loosened. He was gone.

The Fall of Decency

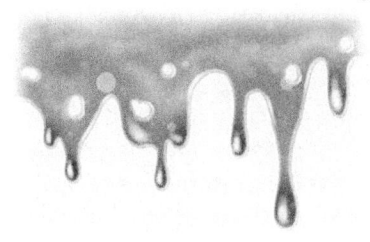

They chased Kevin and Tax for street after street until both men feared their lungs would set ablaze. Their numbers were too much even for Kevin's bodyguard, and so they fled. Now they hid in a multi-story carpark and whispered between a van and a car.

"Do you think they're still out there?"

Tax gave Kevin a withering look and put one finger over his own lips. Kevin looked away and peered through the gap in the concrete barrier which afforded him a miniscule view of the road. When Kevin looked back, Tax had disappeared, and he couldn't help but let out a shocked gasp. There was a crunch of grit on concrete behind him and he instinctively ducked to the sound just in time for a hand axe to swish over his head and connect noisily with the side of the car. Kevin cringed to the ground as the sound of shuffling feet was replaced by grunts and moans. A heavy body dropped on him, and Kevin squirmed so his face was met with the unconscious features of a man who might have

The Growth

been an accountant before the Growth had come to town.

What have we become? he thought sadly.

Tax rolled the man off him as much as possible so Kevin could untangle himself and get to his feet. For a moment, the dripping of blood from Tax's hammer was the only sound.

"They know we're in here," Tax whispered. "That's why they're sticking around."

Kevin responded by picking up the small axe. Against his true nature he had to admit the weapon felt good in his hand. He peeked around the car and saw three men standing on the only ramp leading to ground level. From below he could hear more of the gang noisily searching and calling out to each other.

"I've got an idea," he whispered to Tax who smirked in response.

The heavy work boot bounced off the rear of the Mercedes which had been gathering dust and pigeon shit. Its noise was enough to attract the three men's attention. Kevin had thrown the boot, which he'd removed from Taxs' latest victim, and was initially filled with relief when the trick worked first time. The sound of the three men from the ramp shouting and scuffling their feet closer to where he was hiding soon rid Kevin of any satisfaction. A figure with a knife rushed past the cars he crouched between as the men encircled the Mercedes. Kevin cringed closer to the door he

The Growth

was pressed against and closed his eyes pathetically. The sound of banging on the body work of a car from the other end of the floor suddenly filled the stagnant air. It caused the men to shout more commands and Kevin to sigh in relief knowing his bodyguard was still out there.

"Wait here!" he heard someone say.

Kevin inched forward and saw the man with the knife remained near the Mercedes. The other two had seemingly moved on to investigate the noise Tax had engineered. There was a scraping of metal from the man's knife as he almost lay down to see under the noisy car and its neighbours. Kevin's eyes locked onto the boot he had thrown at the same time as the other man had noticed it. He turned in all directions and Kevin was forced to shrink back into the shadows. Images of the knife pumping in and out of his chest almost brought a gasp from him and he held onto his unsteady breaths in fear they would give him away.

He's going to work out where it's been thrown from!

Kevin could feel himself overheating with stress as the knife scraped into concrete nearer and nearer. He knew part of the plan may include him having to help Tax with the violence yet here he was frozen by fear with the familiar flutter in his bladder.

Move you bastard, move!

The Growth

"Got yer."

Kevin looked up at the figure. A stubbled grin sat atop gaunt features. Filthy sports clothing matched the dirty hand which held up the knife. Kevin's eyes zoned in on the old blood which crusted on the blade. Further evidence of societies descent into chaotic hysteria. A roar of pain echoed from the other side of the parking floor and the knifeman turned to see with a reflex twitch. Kevin threw out his arm clumsily from the position he squatted in. The small axe collided with the opposite car before ricocheting into the knife wielder's inner thigh. Blood spurted forth so violently it hissed at Kevin who let go of the handle in disgust. The word "artery" repeated in his mind with an unhealthy dose of shock. He watched in terror as the man looked down at him with fear and bewilderment. The man slumped to the floor awkwardly, so his face rested on its cold surface. It looked as though he was trying to listen for something, but Kevin couldn't cope with the accusing stare so moved away on cramped legs.

Tax collided with Kevin at the rear of the vehicle and was forced to clamp his hand over the shaking man's whimpering mouth. Kevin's shocked eyes grew wider when seeing the amount of blood on Taxs' face.

"It's not mine," Tax whispered.

Kevin closed his eyes and attempted to control his breaths which were leaving him a lot sooner than he'd like. Tax looked around the car at the dead man with an axe in his leg and understood. He felt sadness for the scientist and a numbness for himself.

How long since I first killed? How many since?

There was shouting from near the ramp in the response to the noisy fight.

"We need to sneak past while they're fussing over the bodies."

The scientist nodded quickly and dumbly like a child learning a hard lesson from their scolding parent. Kevin picked up his bag and hung it on his tense shoulders. He couldn't recall feeling so drained or so defeated. The man with the knife lay in a pond of crimson and Kevin hated him for it.

Look what you made me do, you stupid bastard!

Tax had dragged his two victims into the open so the four men who ran up the ramp rushed straight to them. Two stragglers stopped at the side of the man Kevin had killed but the scientist and his bodyguard had already used the parked cars to sneak past them and down the ramp.

After playing a game of hide and seek of the highest stakes, the two men reached the first floor. From their latest hiding place they could peer down and see the main exit from their concrete prison. A group of at least twenty men and women clowned around and on top of the parked cars, liberated from their normal lives by the end of the world. Scuffles

The Growth

broke out here and there as though it were nothing more than shaking hands and Kevin felt as though he were looking down into a shark tank. There was no way through, and he could hear the men above them getting closer. Tax grimaced and his slab-like head twitched from side to side in an attempt to find an answer to this latest challenge.

"Look," Kevin whispered.

Tax followed his point to the far end of the floor. Through the gap he could see the tops of trees that had been planted in a row in a bid to hide some of the dated architecture the car park presented. They went quickly to the first tree, the noise from the raucous crowd below covered their movements. Tax shook his head at the thin branches within reach, so they moved across to look down at the second tree. Once again, the danger of falling straight through the tree was too great a risk so with ever-increasing doubt they went to the third tree. The men exchanged nervous looks. If they hurdled the barrier and stepped out into oblivion the branches may just hold their weight. Kevin pointed at his chest to show Tax he intended on going first but the bigger man shook his head and threw a leg over the barrier. Kevin watched as he gulped a few unsteady breaths.

It was clear Tax was afraid of heights, yet he had volunteered to go first. Kevin found the man's bravery to be an endless thing of staggering proportions. Tax jumped and hit branches noisily. Kevin's heart missed a beat as Taxs' grip did the same with a branch. Mercifully, Tax managed to hug the trunk with his arms and legs while smaller branches whipped painfully across his face. Kevin realised he wouldn't have had the strength to manage the feat and imagined his own broken body at the foot of the tree. Before he could have doubts the sound of shouts getting closer propelled him until he stood on the outside of the barrier facing Tax. The man in the tree nodded and held out his hand. Kevin was sure he was either going to fall or drag Tax down to the street below but surprisingly his tentative leap ended in nothing more than a grazed shin and awkward proximity to his bodyguard.

The tree creaked and complained as the shout of the mob inside the car park bled from every opening.

"We need to get down right now."

Tax nodded his approval and shifted to the side to show Kevin the best branch to start his nervous descent.

Kevin still hobbled around in a circle of pain as Tax jumped down beside him. The ground gave a small tremor and both men looked at the pavement as though their weight had caused the movement. They froze in place and listened to the raucous hollering of the gang nearby. Tax was about to say something when a chorus of screams erupted from the

The Growth

ground floor level of the car park. The men moved along the side of the wall so they could peer through an open section of the barrier. Tendrils snaked under parked cars to grab hold of the scattering gang. Kevin could see the discarded covering in the road and the hole the Growth had burst through. The form was as thick as the tree they had climbed down but with dozens of arms instead of branches.

Tax turned away in disgust as members of the gang were absorbed by the mass. The stench of melting was already carrying to them, but Kevin couldn't take his eyes off the massacre. Two women jumped up onto the roof of a van and for a moment the Growth focused on easier prey. Kevin felt guilty he couldn't help them even though he knew they would have killed him for his bag just minutes earlier. No, they had brought this on themselves by becoming animals and making so much noise. One of the women let out a panicked whimper and was snatched so quickly from atop the van she smashed through the windscreen of the car next to it before being pulled from sight. This seemed to lend fervour to the other tendrils who converged on the van, becoming one as they did so. Kevin stared like a child watching their first horror movie as the vehicle was overcome. The remaining woman lay on her back and accepted her fate with eyes clamped shut and an anguished cry which was suffocated by the weight of the

The Growth

slimy substance.

Once Kevin had pointed them in the right direction, the men ran as quickly as their legs would allow. They'd been surviving on the bare minimum for days and Tax had finally agreed to take one of the appetite suppressants Kevin had been offering for days. Even so, the men were low on energy and their morale had been drained by the sights they limped away from. The husks of emergency vehicles were scattered throughout their route, grim reminders of the sickening riots which had swept through towns and cities in the face of oncoming death.

We really showed our true faces, Kevin thought wearily as they jogged.

Screams penetrated the air from all directions. Unseen survivors had been hiding out in the ghost town after all. Kevin wondered if the noise which had saved his and Taxs' life had cost others their own. They kept pumping their legs down highstreets in a way which reminded Kevin of pumping air into a punctured tire. They didn't have much left and they were still miles away from the military base where Kevin used to work. The screams stopped and the men slowed to a brisk walk. Kevin pretended not to notice Tax had tears running over his square jaw.

"What's the fucking point?"

Tax had stopped now, and Kevin turned in surprise to see his fearless protector looking

The Growth

utterly defeated.

"People are shit," Tax wept as he wiped tears away with his club of a hand.

Kevin took his glasses off and used the bottom of his jumper to clean them before taking a deep breath and returning them to his nose. It was an action he performed thousands of times before which he often did while embarking on a challenging task. Preventing Tax from giving up when he totally agreed with the man was certainly going to be difficult.

"They wanted to kill us and I'm glad that thing came and got um!"

Kevin nodded slowly and stepped close enough to Tax so he could pat him awkwardly on his tricep.

"I know, mate. I know."

"I don't wanna be killing people!" Tax roared like a wounded animal.

He wiped snot and tears on the back of his sleeve and lost control of a strangled sob that escaped his throat.

"We didn't have a choice, Tax. They were going to kill us."

Tax shot Kevin a look of a scolded child who hasn't fully come around to the idea of leaving their bad mood.

"I've never had a fight in my life and now I've killed someone," he told Tax sadly.

Tax wiped his nose with his cuff.

"Yeah, but he were gonna kill you."

"Exactly, Tax! That's all you did as well."

The Growth

Tax turned away as though seeking time out to mull over the point. Kevin was about to suggest they keep moving when Tax wheeled around.

"Why are we trying to save them?" he spat. "People like that don't deserve it!"

"Not everyone is like that though, mate."

"Feels like it."

Kevin was about to take his glasses off for a clean again when he suddenly recalled the image of the woman with her son.

"What about that kid?"

"What kid?"

"The one with the woman we had tried to talk to."

"She had a knife," Tax pouted.

Kevin held his hands out in a gesture to suggest they were doing the same.

"So they deserve to die too?"

"No."

"So we should try and do this for the good people?"

"Yeah, I suppose."

"Good people like us," Kevin smiled as they set off walking again.

"You're not good?"

"What?"

"You killed a man with an axe, Kevin."

The duo took a few strides before bursts of laughter left them in cynical gusts.

The Pit of Divine Retribution

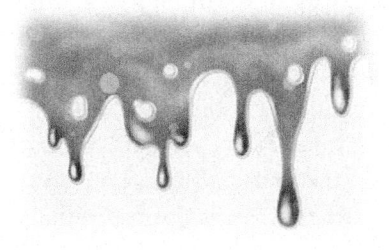

The men had hidden themselves away in the small confines of a local post office. After checking for anything worthwhile, and coming up empty handed, they made painful beds on the floor. As usual Tax fell asleep first and quickly found himself dreaming deeply. The world of his dreams was not a ruinous one, yet there was something skulking in the shadows watching him as he merrily walked down familiar streets. There was a scraping noise which caused Tax to twitch but then his dream showed a house to his right had opened its huge door to him. Two beautiful women stood in the doorway and called his name. Both were different yet shared the same face. They were both Claire Littler, his old high school crush. Except now she was older and more importantly, not repulsed by Tax. In fact, they beckoned him with gestures and giggles which pulled him forwards. His heart sang as he reached them. Their beautiful smiles were the same as he remembered, and they called his name over and over.

The Growth

"Tax... Tax!"

He felt their warm hands on him, and he relaxed into the feeling of love sickness.

"Tax!"

They pulled on his arms, and he was glad of their contact. Tax tried to focus on their faces, but the beauty had gone now and the more he tried to focus the more their features looked like rain-streaked windows. The touch he had been enjoying moments before was now becoming uncomfortable and he emitted a snort which transcended both his waking and dreaming state.

"For God's sake, Tax!" they screamed.

Except it wasn't Claire Littler screaming, it was Kevin. Tax opened his eyes in terror to see hooded men dragging Kevin outside. He struggled groggily against the two men who held his arms behind his back. Kevin disappeared from view just as another hooded man planted his boot into Taxs' face. Bright sparks were chased away by darkness, and he returned to his dreams.

*

Emma was being followed. She'd taken to talking to herself and it was during one of her outbursts when she heard the sound of debris being crunched under the boot of another. Emma didn't turn to look, instead she angled

The Growth

her direction towards a side street with a slight change in her walking pace. Emma planned on sprinting away once she rounded the next corner but there was more commotion from behind which indicated her pursuer knew they'd been noticed and no longer cared for discretion.

Shit!

The opening to the side street was close but the shuffle of a misplaced step was closer. Emma burst out running and was several strides down what now appeared to be no more than an alleyway before she heard the clattering feet of the chase. Shuttered doors flashed by as Emma picked up the pace. A ten-foot fence was fast becoming the finish line and Emma didn't know if she'd be able to get up and over it without getting caught. Twenty metres from the fence and Emma made the decision to go for it and accelerated to a full-on sprint.

"Where are you going, bitch?" a voice called from behind her.

Emma jolted to a stop and turned to acknowledge the voice.

Change of plan, she seethed.

The two men nearly bumped into each as they jostled to a stop in the narrow alleyway. They both had their hoods up which were marked with white paint.

Some bullshit gang.

Emma threw her bag off and switched to

her comfortable fighting stance. Her back heaved for a few moments before returning to the stillness her stamina allowed for. The men grinned at each other and exchanged looks of amusement. Emma smiled.

"Which one of you called me a bitch?"

The scruffy men seemed confused to be asked a question rather than be met with begging.

"Well?"

The smaller of the two stepped forward. He had a gingery beard and was sickeningly pale.

"I did, sinner," he spat while jabbing a finger at his chest.

"*Sinner*? You're the one's chasing me."

"We're doing His work," the other man called in a sing-song voice.

Emma sighed loud enough for both men to be offended by it. It stood to reason there would be a clamour towards religion as the world went to shit. She pointed at the closest man.

"Why don't you come here, and I'll show you who the real bitch is."

The man smirked and showed a flash of yellow teeth. He pulled a knife from his belt and walked confidently towards his prey. Emma hit him with two rapid left jabs which popped his nose. She registered the man's shocked eyes as she quickly followed up with a right cross to his jaw. He crumpled to one knee

The Growth

as though proposing and dropped the blade. Emma moved the hood and grabbed a handful of her attacker's greasy hair. The other man took an uncertain step forward so Emma pulled at her captive who squealed in pain.

"Uh, uh," she warned the second man.

He was bigger than the man she had felled, and his face changed from surprise to anger. However, the moment he took another step, Emma struck her captive on his broken nose. The smaller man squealed in pain.

"Please!" he begged as much to his partner as to Emma.

The second man stopped but fixed Emma with a defiant stare. She responded by striking her captive once more and waving her bloodied fist towards him.

"Ok, ok. Just stop," he growled.

Emma pulled on the greasy hair a little more and sneered at the men.

"What if I told you I was doing Her work?" she mocked them.

The man who hung back narrowed his eyes as though seeing her for the first time. His face scrunched up as though trying to look at something through thick fog.

"I know you. You're Emma Holt!"

Emma didn't reply. Instead she recalled the roar from the Olympic crowd. She could hear if she closed her eyes but now was not the time.

"Get the fuck out of here," she screamed

as she threw her captive onto the floor.

The man was helped to his feet, and both scurried away with hurt glances over their shoulders in a way which told Emma they could live forever and never tell a soul of their embarrassment. She watched as they turned left out of the alleyway. It was back the way she had come from, but she had been walking aimlessly for too long. Now though, she had a purpose. Emma decided she was going to follow the snakes back to whichever rock they had crawled from under and inflict pain on the whole nest.

*

The pressure of gravity dragged Tax from the darkness, and it took a furious bout of blinking for him to comprehend his predicament. His back had a steel girder biting into it. His arms had been pulled either side of the girder and bound at the wrists with rope. Tax was sitting on a platform no bigger than an average dining table with his face leaning towards a drop of around seventy feet. His view was of an abandoned construction yard which he observed from within the skeleton of a never-to-be finished hotel. Machinery reflected the last of the day's sun and although his binding wouldn't allow him to see, Tax

The Growth

knew something else lurked down below. He stood on unsteady legs and winced at the cramp in his arms and the blood crusted on the side of his face.

"I'm here, Tax."

"Kevin?"

Kevin nodded, realised Tax couldn't see him, and cleared his throat nervously.

"Yeah, I'm behind you."

"Where are they?"

"They're below us praying," Kevin replied in a voice just loud enough for Tax to hear.

"Praying?"

"Yeah."

"Jesus."

"Not sure he's factoring into it to be honest with you, mate."

Tax looked back out to the machinery and as the wind changed, he heard a wet sound from below.

"What's down there, Kev?"

"A massive drainage pit that's full of the Growth."

Tax didn't reply. Instead he looked from side to side for any clue of escape. The moment he realised there were no tools to free him, Kevin spoke again.

"They're going to throw us into the pit. They're freaks, mate. Saying something about being a brotherhood and cleansing the land."

Kevin was losing control of his voice, the tone and speed of speech betraying his fear.

The Growth

Tax took a breath and enjoyed the freshness of the air at their current height. His voice was level and almost robotic.

"How many?"

"Ten, maybe?"

"Maybe?"

"I dunno, Tax! We're gonna die here!"

"Calm down."

"...Sorry."

Tax rapidly clenched and unclenched his fists to try and stimulate blood flow.

"Are you tied up as tight as me?"

"No."

"Can you free yourself?" Tax asked excitedly.

"I'm not tied up."

"What do you mean you're not tied up?"

Tax heard Kevin shuffle uncomfortably on the wooden board behind him.

"I pissed myself, ok?" Kevin wept. "They laughed and called me a coward and just left me up here with you."

"And nobody's guarding us?"

"There's nowhere to go, Tax!"

"Get me untied right now!" Tax hissed.

"I can't."

Tax wriggled in an attempt to fix Kevin with a cold stare. Instead he clonked his prominent brow against the steel he was tied to. The blow snapped him into changing tact.

"I can protect you."

Kevin sat cross legged and defeated and

The Growth

wiped tears away so that he could stare at Taxs' bound paws. He wanted to believe Tax, but he couldn't will his legs to move. The shame of urine burns were a constant reminder of the coward within him. Chanting from below grew louder with every wasted second.

"Come on, Kev," Tax begged.

The chanting became whoops of joy and Kevin was put in mind of hyenas. He clenched his jaw in anger and to the flashbacks of the hooded men laughing at his display of cowardice and fear. Tax was about to issue another plea when he felt the ropes shift slightly as Kevin tried to free him. He felt hot tears of his own as he nodded thankfully to himself.

The chanting below suddenly ceased, and Kevin fired a nervous glance over his shoulder. Tax felt Kevin let go of the rope.

"No, no. Keep going."

Kevin fumbled at the ropes and Tax felt them give slightly.

"Come on, come on," Kevin muttered.

"Well you do surprise me," Michael Applewood announced from behind Kevin.

Kevin flinched as two sets of hands dragged him away from Tax.

"No!" he screamed.

"Leave him alone, you bastards!" Tax roared.

"Oh, we'll get to you," Michael smirked at the bound hands.

The Growth

Brother Gary and Brother Mark pinned Kevin to the floor as Michael stood over him. Tax could hear at least six other sets of feet enter the area via the dusty concrete stairs.

"We have good tidings to bring you both," Michael announced. "After much singing to our Lord and saviour we have reached a judgement to help you right your wrongs."

Tax moved his hands as much as he could within the slack that his friend had created. Kevin stared in dumbfounded fear at the crazed religious nut who was practically frothing at the mouth each time he passed by, whirling around the scene theatrically. Both men holding his wrists in place were nodding enthusiastically and Kevin felt the chilled knot in his stomach which told him the end was near.

"The Growth is hungry for the souls of sinners, and it is our duty to feed the cleansing beast below. Fear not, sinners. This change is for the good of humanity and you will finally be contributing something positive."

Tax didn't understand the strange man but knew enough to realise Kevin had been right to be afraid. They really were going to throw them off the building. The height was more than enough to kill a person without the added deadly presence of the Growth in the pit below. The sermon continued.

"Once marked you will take the flight of change and fulfil a role which will finally put

The Growth

your troubled souls at peace."

Michael swirled around once more and paused. He looked at the loyal faces around him and then at the wretched man on the floor.

"Where is brother Damien?"

The hooded men looked at each other and then back to their leader.

"He went below to get the blessed fluid so the sinners could be marked," Brother Nick called out.

Michael smiled at the devotion of his men. The blessed fluid was actually black metal paint, but the conviction of Brother Nick's words was pleasing.

"Can you go and assist Brother Damien?" Michael clapped his hands together. "Perhaps he is having trouble placing the blessed fluid."

Brother Nick nodded and rushed back down the staircase. Tax continued to work his hands from the rope as forcefully as he dared. Deep down he knew he wouldn't have time to free himself.

Pandemonium On the Fifth Floor.

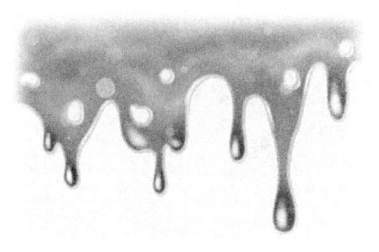

Emma was in the process of dragging the unconscious man behind some crates when she heard footsteps approaching at pace.

"Brother Damien?"

Emma gently laid Damien down and waited for the footsteps to get closer. She'd followed her two attackers through the streets and watched from across the road as they explained their failure to a hooded man who hugged them warmly before escorting them out of sight. Emma had been both repulsed and angered by the weird cult shit she'd stumbled upon but had forced herself to follow the men inside.

"Brother Damien?"

Emma charged the man as he looked down at his fallen "brother." She hit Brother Nick with everything she had, enraged by their earlier meeting. Elbows and forearms hit the man in his sternum as Emma powered her way forward. Nick reached for her but too late. His

The Growth

last step was out onto fresh air, so he grasped desperately for the barrier his body had breached. The man's hand reached nothing but flimsy red tape he pulled to his death. Emma shuffled back from the edge as the sickening crunch of something bursting came back up to her.

Tax heard the screech of someone falling from the building which set his mind racing as well as evoke pandemonium behind him.

"Brought some friends, have we?" Michael shrieked.

Hands pulled at Kevin's legs before he had a chance to respond.

"Let him fly to the pit," Michael ordered. "You two go and check below."

Tax heard running footsteps and then the sound of Kevin being dragged by his ankles towards the edge.

"No please!"

Tax began to frantically attempt to pull his arms from their binding.

"Get off him!"

The ropes burned his skin and plucked the hairs from his arms but Tax roared defiance at the situation until his left hand was released in a motion that almost dislocated his shoulder. He brought his reunited limb to his front just as a hooded figure grabbed hold of it and attempted to pull it back towards the rope. Kevin's screams were getting closer to Tax and then he heard a woman call out from the staircase.

Emma stood at the top of the steps and took in the insanity at play. For a brief moment the men simply looked at the blood dripping from the piece of rebar in her hand. Michael locked eyes with Emma, who in turn looked to Kevin on the floor. Two hooded men edged slowly towards Emma, and Michael smirked in a way which brought anger up in her like poisonous vomit. Then all hell broke loose as she ran between them, swinging the thick metal bar while releasing a battle cry which tore pigeons from the roof of the hotel. The man attempting to control Tax let go of his arm and moved out of sight to help the others. Moments later he bounced to the floor in front of Tax's leg with blood pouring from his ear. Tax instinctively kicked out at the fallen man; his boot connected painfully with the man's ribs who gasped at the contact.

"Get up!" Emma shouted at Kevin.

There was frantic fumbling at the ropes and Tax was suddenly free. Kevin came and stood on the platform with wild eyes. A hooded man ran to him, and they began to grapple before Tax pulled the man off his friend. He hit the hooded man with a right hook full of frustration and murderous intent which staggered him, so he was sent screaming over the edge. Emma was half tackled by two men and Michael lent his weight so the rolling scrum of bodies soon collided with Kevin who

The Growth

staggered backwards towards the seventy-foot drop. Tax took a quick step on the shaky platform and grabbed a handful of Kevin's coat to halt his momentum. A hand immediately hit Tax on the side of his head which made his ears ring violently. Kevin kicked out at the man who had thrown the punch, producing a yelp like a wounded dog. The mass of bodies writhed and fought as the platform shuddered underneath their shuffling feet.

Tax threw his elbow into the throat of the nearest hooded man who gurgled and fell to his knees. For the first time he got a look at their saviour and was so astounded he stopped fighting and was promptly punched in his mouth for the lapse in concentration. Kevin jumped on the man's back and stared at Tax with pleading eyes.

"Wake up, Tax!"

Tax snapped out of his stupor and wrestled with yet another hooded figure while shouting at Kevin.

"It's Emma bloody Holt!"

Tax was beaming through bloodied teeth as though Kevin should know what he was talking about. Emma had lost her weapon in the tangle of limbs and began to throw vicious uppercuts and hooks in an attempt to free herself. Tax enthusiastically began to mimic the boxer's movements while Kevin was thrown onto the platform. A rush of legs surrounded him, and he had just enough time to feel the vibrations through the wood before the sound of splintering made his stomach flip.

"Stop! Stop!"

Then the platform fell from beneath them.

Fallout

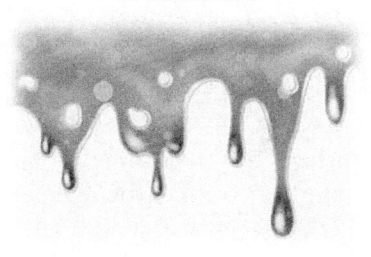

Kevin felt as though he had awoken with his head underwater. Every scream was muffled and his whole body was surrounded by pressure which moved all around him. He began to panic as the movement confirmed he was underneath at least three people with his arms pinned to his side. Kevin squirmed but the broken body beneath him prohibited him from getting enough purchase. His head was free so he turned it left but could see nothing but the dust which the collapse had kicked up. When Kevin turned right, he saw a man's broken body which had bloodied bones sticking through ripped clothing. The body's head had been crushed under the weight of the collapse, a smashed melon which bared its meat for all to witness. Kevin tried to scream but the weight of others constricted it to a crazed wheeze.

Emma heard the steady dripping of a leaky shower and the occasional cough from her neighbour.

No that's not right. Wake up!

The Growth

Emma opened her eyes and looked at the small puddle her facial wound had created. She dabbed at the area and of course it was her prominent brow which had been cut. It made sense for it to be the troublesome area which had blemished her record and caused her career to stutter. Emma would have laughed cynically if she weren't wrapped over a pile of bricks. Her stomach was scraped and tender but there was the cough again. She looked over to see the big man who had been tied up being strangled by whom she presumed to be the leader of this particular circus. Emma ignored the ringing in her ears as she rose on shaky legs. A figure kicked out at her from the floor, and she turned to retaliate until realising it was the last act of a man impaled on a length of timber. He coughed red bubbles and fell silent so Emma could limp onwards in an attempt to save the big man once more.

Tax watched the black spots in the corners of his vision rather than the curled lips of his attacker. He remembered falling and falling as the scaffold platform had buckled, stopped, and buckled again, until they came to a rest three floors lower than where they had started their descent. Tax held the wrists of the hands seeking to extinguish him, but his strength had a dream quality to it as though he were fighting below the waves. He turned his head slightly as he gave up and saw Kevin squirming against the broken bodies which had insulated him against serious injury. Hands grabbed at his terrified friend and the sight ignited a rage in him. Tax grunted and wriggled against the strangulation.

"Die, sinner!" Michael heaved.

Then a punch he never saw coming was launched from behind. A right hook exploded into Michael's face which sent him rolling off Tax. The impact of the punch broke his jaw horrifically, so it hung like a door with a bust hinge. Michael held the bottom of his face carefully as though handling a wounded bird and shuffled away on his backside. Tax rolled to his feet and immediately set about dragging bodies off Kevin. Any that clawed at him were swiftly dealt with by brutal punches and elbows. Emma ignored Michael who cowered with his back against a broken wall and moved to look over the edge for a way out. A mound of bulldozed earth was directly below them, but it sloped to the pit where the Growth bubbled in a constant state of agitation. Emma was judging the height of the fall to the slope when Michael jumped onto her back causing her legs to buckle and send them both over the edge.

Tax watched in horror as Emma Holt fell from sight and quickly pulled Kevin to his feet.

"We've got to go help her!"

Kevin nodded silently as he tried to gulp air into his bruised chest. He watched Tax drop from view and followed in a trance. It was only

The Growth

when he was in the air that he realised he'd misjudged the height and he came down painfully on his heels, rolling his right ankle in the process. Emma untangled herself from Michael's limbs and the winded man rolled slowly away from her with shaking hands still holding his jaw together. Tax stumbled down the slope to Emma's side as the sound of shouting came from nearby. Yet more hooded figures ran around the base of the building. Kevin rubbed his ankle and wobbled to his feet while releasing a hiss of pain.

"There's too many of them," Emma muttered.

Michael laughed softly which produced bloodied drool from his broken mouth. It was a laugh cut short when one of his followers was suddenly snatched by the Growth and hefted into the air. All watched as the man landed in a broken pile atop the middle of the mass. There was no scream as the body disappeared quickly like a seagull consumed by an oil spill. The remaining seven hooded men froze in place as they realised their noise had put them on the Growth's radar. Tax and Emma turned slowly to watch Kevin limping quietly down the slope.

"Get him out of here," Emma whispered to Tax.

Michael gestured for help and two of his disciples crept closer. Tax took one step towards them, but Emma grabbed his shoulder.

"Do you have a reason to live?" she

The Growth

quietly asked.

Tax looked at the boxer's hand and then at Kevin who attempted a brave smile through the pain of his twisted ankle.

"I do, yeah."

The hooded men were pulling Michael to his feet as the rest inched closer to Emma and Tax.

"Then get him out of here," Emma prompted.

Tax was about to protest when Emma charged Michael and delivered a kick to his gut. Michael folded up and pulled one of his followers with him. Incensed, the group of followers raced to Michael's aid. Emma was dragged back but Tax waded in and delivered hammer fists to anyone in his way. Kevin limped forward with his eyes fixed on the pit.

"Look out!" he called as loudly as he dared.

The nearest man who was attempting to escort Michael away from the conflict was grabbed around both ankles and fell screaming to the floor. For a moment he held fast onto Michael's legs until another disciple kicked him in the face so their leader would be spared. The unconscious man was dragged along the ground like a bag of soil as a further tentacle-like length groped for further prey. Emma watched as her nearest opponent was snatched away with smoke searing from his burning trousers.

The Growth

"Go!" she screamed at Tax.

Michael was being dragged away by two of his men while Kevin limped in the opposite direction. Emma was dropped to the floor by a cuffing blow to her temple and Tax had his nose broken as he dragged her back to her feet. He headbutted the offender through watering eyes in an act of swift retribution. The sound of ruined cartilage only matched by the squeal from the man. The Growth rushed over ground towards the mele.

"Go!" Emma screamed.

Tax looked at Emma who swayed like a drunk street fighter. There were three hooded men willing to give their lives so their leader could scurry away. Tax thought he and Emma could take them but noticed the Growth snaking closer as it branched out. Sunlight reflected off the membrane of a lance which was attracted by Kevin's stumbling progress. Emma scooped up a large rock and threw it at the men who all flinched away. The two fighters locked eyes. Tax recognised the expression on the boxer's face as one he had worn many times. It was the mask of self-destruction which only the wearer had the right to remove. He let out a long breath and nodded. Tax ran to save Kevin but not before throwing a brick of his own which split the nearest man's head open.

Kevin could see the Growth moving for him in his peripheral vision and knew he

The Growth

wouldn't be fast enough to get clear. Tax grabbed him around the waist and half carried him away with the strength of a rugby player. Kevin hopped on his good leg and saw the opening in the fence they were headed for. The part of the Growth giving chase suddenly changed course back to the din of the fight.

"Wait, wait," Kevin hissed.

Tax dragged him through the opening and onto the pavement before he allowed his friend to stop his progress. They watched in sadness from the side-lines as Emma fought her final bout. They shielded their eyes to the sun to better see the silhouettes which danced death steps. Tax nodded approval as Emma punched swiftly to knock down two attackers. A figure would suddenly disappear from view as the Growth snatched them away until only Emma and one hooded man remained.

"I can't watch," Kevin's voice cracked as he hobbled away.

Tax nodded his appreciation as Emma's silhouette continued to bob and weave. He turned to follow Kevin with tears in his eyes. Emma had fought so they could live, and he refused to watch her fall. Much better to remember the elegant fighter bravely throwing punches for all eternity.

You Have Reached Your Destination

They travelled in silence until it was too dark to do so. Taxs' eyes were swollen from his broken nose and every step he had to fight the urge to blow it. The journey was slow going due to Kevin's ankle, but they made steady progress out of destroyed towns and shuffled along empty rural roads. Out in the country it was almost possible to forget the Growth existed, yet every farmhouse they struck upon was abandoned. After an uncomfortable night in one such property they walked for most of the following day until Kevin suddenly stopped and pointed at a long row of trees which snaked off to the left. The men stood surrounded by fields which stretched away for miles to the horizon. Tax shielded his eyes to the sun so he could better see why his friend had stopped.

"We take the next left for the entrance to the base. We'll get to the main gate after about half a mile."

The Growth

Tax grinned and nodded enthusiastically. After several brushes with death they had somehow made it.

"We did it!"

Kevin sniffed and produced a trembling smile full of emotion. The unlikely duo embraced in the middle of the road, only the sound of their weeping could be heard over the distant calls of crows.

Kevin fished into his bag and retrieved his outdated identification card before placing the lanyard over his head. Tax looked at the badge hanging from Kevin's neck and squinted at the old photograph of his friend.

"What are you going to say?"

Kevin self-consciously turned the badge, so the unflattering picture was no longer on display.

"Well, first we need to get them to let us inside."

"Why wouldn't they?"

Kevin set off walking and Tax fell in at his side.

"It's been years since I was here," Kevin admitted. "I shouldn't even have this I.D anymore."

"I thought you worked here?"

"I did."

"You left?"

Kevin wanted to tell Tax everything. The failed experiments, the shame and disgrace he left under. Tax stared at him expectantly and

The Growth

Kevin felt pangs of guilt for selling his bodyguard a dream which was steeped in lies. It would work though; he was sure of it. All he hoped was there would be no faces from his past to ridicule him before he had even delivered his idea.

"Kev?"

"Yeah, I needed a change," Kevin forced a smile. "Come on, let's get going."

The main gate was fifteen feet tall and chained shut. Kevin had expected it to be manned by armed guards but there was no sign of life. The perimeter fence stretched away and out of sight, so the men stood with their hands on their hips and squinted through the chain links before them.

"Is that a plane?"

"Yeah," Kevin confirmed. "There's an old airfield over that way, but it wasn't in use when I worked here."

The men fell into silence as they searched out movement from the distant buildings. Kevin noticed rows of medical tents near the canteen area and took it as a sign the base was still being used.

"Is this the only way in?"

"We could try the south entrance but it's a bit of a walk and will probably be locked up like this one."

Tax craned his neck to look at the razor wire which ran along the top of the fence. A brief flashback of misspent youth forced a

The Growth

smirk.

"Don't even think about it," Kevin cautioned.

Tax took his coat off in response and stepped towards the nearest fence post.

"It hurts your hands but if you're strong enough you can climb it."

"No. No way! What about the razor wire?"

Tax waved his coat at Kevin and grabbed a handful of the fence. He put a foot into the post and boosted himself up. After a few moments Tax repeated the movement until he was in a position to quickly throw his coat from over his shoulder. A few attempts later the material was over the metal deterrent and Tax was pulling himself over, so he sat astride the fence.

"Shit!" he hissed as his inner thigh was punctured.

"You alright?"

Tax ignored Kevin and rubbed at his left hand with the concentrating look of a child searching for a splinter.

"How am I supposed to get over that?"

Tax looked at Kevin as though he'd asked something beyond ridiculous.

"Same way I did."

"I'm not as strong as you."

"I know that," Tax giggled. "I'll stay here and pull you up."

Kevin didn't like his chances but what

The Growth

choice did he have. To come all this way and be defeated by a fence was unacceptable. He launched his bag over the fence in one attempt which gave him renewed confidence. Tax smiled down at him and nodded as though impressed.

There was a sudden noise which snapped Kevin's head around to the trees behind them. He assumed a branch had been noisily broken off, but the sound evolved into the distant report of a rifle. Kevin quickly turned to see Tax holding his stomach, his face already a ghostly white. The men looked into each other's eyes as Tax raised a blood smeared hand.

"No," was all Kevin could manage.

Tax toppled off the fence and landed heavily in the long grass they'd been so desperate to reach only moments earlier.

"Tax!"

Kevin ripped his lanyard off and began waving it hysterically in the air. He hoped the sniper had a skilled spotter.

"Don't shoot! Don't shoot!"

Kevin continued to wave his I.D card in the air and braced himself for the bullet.

"Tax!" he screamed again.

A new sound emerged from the distance and Kevin saw two jeeps racing towards him.

*

The Growth

The medical tents Kevin had observed were in fact only being used to keep extra munitions safe and dry. They had raced straight past the stacks of boxes and Tax had instead been thrown on a stretcher and rushed through the main doors and down a dimly lit corridor. Kevin had slipped on some of his friend's blood and watched helplessly as he was stopped from following Tax into surgery. Soldiers ushered him into a small room which he recognised as an old colleague's office. A dull photograph of Professor Kane and his wife was the only company Kevin had and rather than sitting on the chair he'd been offered he instead sat on the cold floor with the wall to his back. His legs were rendered useless with a sickening anxiety for his friend and the nausea kept him in a constant state of discomfort. Fatigue eventually overwhelmed all other senses and Kevin's eyes remained shut for longer after each blink until he succumbed to the heavy sleep of exhaustion.

The sound of the office door opening, and shutting didn't bring Kevin any closer to the waking world but the noise from a man grunting as he sat in the nearby chair woke him with a start. Kevin squirmed away the painful numbness one gets from sleeping on the floor. The man on the chair observed him like someone staring into a small fire. Kevin rubbed his eyes and noticed the insignia on the older man's uniform. He attempted to stand on numb legs. The man tiredly waved his hand in a gesture that told Kevin to relax and stay on the floor. He had thin grey hair and features which suggested a life of being outdoors. His long legs suggested he was tall when standing but what Kevin couldn't move on from was how much the man looked like his late father. The man in the chair self-consciously rubbed his stubble which was crowned by a heavily brushed moustache.

"You'll have to excuse my appearance but things like shaving have gone out the bloody window. I've just spent an hour arguing with an American called Major Glover who wanted us to secure him a live sample of the Growth if you can believe that!"

Kevin nodded dumbly. Now he had reached the base to discuss his creation, he found his tongue was unwilling to cooperate with his racing mind. The man shuffled uncomfortably in the office chair which gave out an embarrassing squeak. A furrowed brow was directed at it briefly before the man returned his gaze to Kevin.

"I'm Brigadier Thomas and I suppose you could say I'm in charge of this circus."

Kevin pointed at his own chest like a caveman.

"Kevin."

Brigadier Thomas retrieved Kevin's I.D badge from his combat pants and held it up.

"I know who you are but why are you

The Growth

here?"

Kevin hesitated again as he didn't remember giving up the lanyard.

Maybe in the jeep?

Brigadier Thomas leaned forward as though talking to a small child.

"Kevin? It looks like your friend is going to live but you have some explaining to do."

Kevin found his jaw was quivering uncontrollably.

"Bullet wasn't a problem apparently, but the infection is trying its damnedest to snuff him out."

Brigadier Thomas let out a hearty guffaw as though relishing the fortitude of man.

"Tax is going to live?"

"Tax?"

"My friend," Kevin croaked.

"Tax," the Brigadier tried the word in his mouth one last time before shaking his head.

Kevin watched the tall man unfold from the chair and walk wearily to the desk where he poked at various bits of stationary.

"I'm sure you can understand that I'm a very busy man," the Brigadier smiled without warmth. "Especially these days."

Kevin tried to moisten his parched mouth to no avail and the Brigadier, clearly a man used to a speech or two, continued.

"We've had a few intruders these past few weeks but you're the first ex-employee we've seen."

The Growth

There was something in the tone and language the Brigadier used which told Kevin he was on borrowed time. It seemed the military leader saw conversations in the same way he saw conflicts. A battle he simply must win.

"You were seconds away from being shot. I had assumed you were simply more civvies looking for shelter, but my men tell me you have an idea to hurt this beast?"

The Brigadier aimed his contempt at Kevin to show he found the notion of this being true as completely preposterous.

Kevin began to worry about the welfare of those who had attempted to access the military base before him but was forced to push the thoughts to the back of his mind. The Brigadier had perfectly set him up to pitch his idea so he could not hesitate any longer.

"As you know I worked in the scientific wing here for many years," Kevin began.

The military man said nothing and simply stared at Kevin until he continued.

"Yeah, so ok. I came up with a formula which was initially developed to combat chemical warfare, but it became more destructive than the bombs themselves."

"So it's unstable?" the Brigadier cut in.

Kevin mentally stumbled. He had assumed his idea would be met by a captive audience, desperate for an answer to their prayers. Yet here he was, hastily cobbling his

The Growth

sentences together in front of a career soldier in a poorly lit dusty office.

"Well, of course, yes. But it's that unstable nature which is its greatest strength in this situation."

The Brigadier pulled a face, so Kevin fumbled in his bag for his journal. He began thumbing to the pages to find his calculations.

"I think with a big enough quantity we can-"

"Not possible, Kevin."

"What do you mean?"

Brigadier Thomas moved to the window and spoke to Kevin with his back to him. For the first time Kevin could see soldiers rushing around outside.

"You're too late, I'm afraid. For now, this island is lost so we have to get out while we still have a chance."

This island?

Kevin was astonished to hear the country already being reduced to something smaller to take the edge off the guilt.

"You're leaving?"

"For now, yes," the Brigadier turned to face him.

"But the people need you!"

"The people?"

Brigadier waved his hands so violently, Kevin thought he may be struck.

"What do you think we've been doing since we got word from the powers that be,

The Growth

hmm?"

Kevin felt his face flush again and the Brigadier continued.

"We've transported thousands of survivors by plane and ship until the airports and ports became overrun."

Brigadier Thomas thumped his hand down on the desk.

"And we bloody well lost thousands of good men and women doing it!"

Kevin began to mumble an apology, but the Brigadier wasn't done with him yet.

"Scores of loyal soldiers wiped out by that thing was bad enough but when civilians began to ambush my men."

His face was bright red with emotion, and he shook his head so hard it made Kevin believe it may never stop.

"You come here with a bloody diary and half a story about a failed experiment?"

Brigadier Thomas trailed off and clapped his hands together as though closing an invisible book on such matters. When he began to talk again it was in a tired, almost robotic tone.

"We leave for Germany in two days. I'll have one of my men brief you and then you can go and wait with your friend. I suggest you keep this nonsense to yourself because you will find a dangerous lack of patience from a battle-weary soldier."

With that the Brigadier left Kevin alone in

The Growth

an office which belonged in the past with the rest of his work.

Operation Breakout

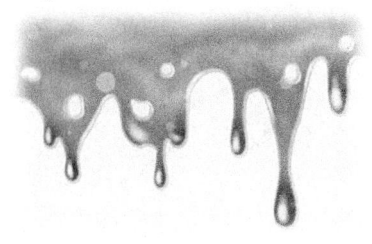

The army medics had saved Taxs' life with an ease approaching boredom. Once the injured man was stable, they had resumed packing up equipment in readiness for evacuation. Tax was monitored briefly when it was time to change the bag of antibiotics which were being pumped into him. Kevin sat numbly by his friend's side like a deflated balloon. The familiar sensation of feeling a failure and a fraud were crushing him and even the news that Tax had recovered enough to make the flight with the medical team had raised only the most polite of smiles. Tax for his part had drifted in and out of consciousness and now Kevin knew his bodyguard was out of the worst, he was glad of it. How could he explain their perilous journey had been for nothing? What could he say to make Tax understand the military had chosen a different weapon to attack the Growth with?

A robotic man, who didn't introduce himself, had briefed Kevin on the basics of Operation Breakout directly after his doomed

The Growth

conversation with Brigadier Thomas. Kevin had sat in silence as vague statements regarding the evacuation were relayed to him. He'd been lost in his own despair and barely listened until the soldier mentioned the gas which would be dropped across the UK once the base had been evacuated. Kevin had voiced scepticism of gas being able to do anything more than surface damage, but the man had dismissed these doubts by simply telling him there had been seriously encouraging and successful field tests. The man wore the same expressions which Brigadier Thomas had so Kevin had swallowed down his ideas in fear of further torment and ridicule. Nor did he mention the morality of gassing those who remained behind.

Presently, he sat and guarded Tax because it was the only thing he could think to do with his time. Small food parcels and bottled water sporadically arrived but Kevin's appetite was miniscule. He stayed hydrated and continued to watch over his friend. Tax occasionally tried to sit up but after a pained smile at his travelling companion he always sagged back down into his pillows where sleep would quickly consume him. The medical team worked in silence as they methodically dismantled various pieces of equipment and moved it into the corridor. From there soldiers would take it away to the waiting aircraft carrier. Kevin sank further into his chair and watched all with eyes grown heavy through stress and exhaustion. Soon even the squeaks of boots on the linoleum floor couldn't prevent him from drifting off to the same state as the man on the bed next to him.

His mother called to him. A voice filtering through the deep water of sleep which woke Kevin with a start. Disorientated, he looked around the empty room with the sensation of his own name echoing in his mind. Kevin couldn't tell if someone had actually shouted his name in the waking world and looked at the door to the corridor expecting someone to barge through. Nobody appeared so he rubbed his face groggily and turned to check on Tax. To Kevin's horror the bed which Tax had been sleeping in was gone. He bolted up in shock and rushed through plastic partitions feeling more desperate with each step. The large room was empty save for a few items not deemed worthy for transport. Kevin swallowed back fear and wondered if he had been deemed unworthy too. He rushed to the corridor but there was no sign of life there either.

"Hello?" he called and immediately felt foolish.

A distant drone entered Kevin's consciousness and he immediately set off running for the exit.

The plane. They're leaving without me!

Each corridor which Kevin raced down was empty and the despair became all-consuming panic. He barrelled through a fire exit into the cool night. The droning sound had

The Growth

a higher pitch to it now and Kevin ran around the building to see the plane bouncing down the overgrown runway as it searched for take-off speed. Kevin thought of movies where the plane would be caught by a hero on a motorbike, but his rational mind told him his fate was sealed. He froze to the spot and watched as the plane's blinking red light moved up as though driving uphill. Except the light kept moving up into the darkness, searching for the altitude it needed to take it to Germany.

The cold seeping through his jeans made Kevin realise he had dropped to his knees. His mind continued to race even if his legs had given up. Had they left him behind on purpose? Why take Tax if that were true? Was it just a stupid mistake? The plane's lights disappeared behind low clouds and Kevin's guts grew cold with a sudden realisation. He thought of the briefing he'd received. The next planes he'd see overhead would be dropping dangerous gas onto their own country. Onto him.

Kevin closed his eyes and visualised his journal which sat in the bag he'd left in the medical room. He thought of the underground science wing in the bunker below his feet.

Maybe it was meant to be, he thought.

Kevin sprang into action. First, he was going to retrieve his journal, then he was going to get as many supplies down into the labs as

The Growth

possible. Who knew what he could cook up down there.

*

The underground tube station had been severely damaged by the Growth's early movements. It had largely collapsed in on itself, but Clive and Amy had found a route through a small tunnel to a damaged utility room. The pair usually just used it as a walk-in storage area to keep anything useful they found but weren't able to carry around with them. They didn't sleep in the room either because the rats often found them, and it wasn't wise to stay in one place for more than a few nights. Since Clive had been saved by Amy, she had been rigidly strict with this rule. Until now. Clive pulled his knees to his chest and shuffled his bum on the uncomfortable floor. He looked at Amy's back as she fussed over their guest. She had cut a lot of her hair off recently, but it had been long and blonde when she had swept him away from the fighting. He missed Amy's long hair because it reminded him of his mum and sister who he missed even more. His saviour wasn't much taller than he was and when Clive had asked her age, Amy had laughed and told him she was ancient. Clive was fairly sure she was at least thirty.

"Are you still sulking?" she asked him now.

The Growth

Clive caught himself pouting and quickly moved his expression to default before Amy turned around.

"We shouldn't stay here," he told her.

Amy looked at the ten-year-old boy who had become a welcome distraction from all the devastation. He was the most honest human Amy had ever been in the company of and keeping him alive had become the only thing she had left. She smiled at his grumpy face and the mess of brown hair he refused to let her cut; even when she'd cut her own. Clive's tracksuit pants were too big for him, and he had to hold onto the waistband whenever running was required to stop them from falling down. Sadly, they ran a lot. Amy tried to find better clothes for both of them, but the boy never complained about it. Food, boredom, and no video games on the other hand were a constant gripe which Amy had to endure.

"You know why we have to stay here, mate."

Clive rolled his eyes.

"I'm starving."

Amy smirked and pointed at the large shopping bag in the corner of the room.

"Pick one tin."

Clive's face turned to pure joy and Amy felt her stomach knot with a mixture of love and heartbreak. She turned and looked down at their guest who lay unconscious on a bundle of tattered blankets.

The Growth

"What's your story, hmm?"

They'd found the athletic looking woman crawling slowly along the pavement near their current location. Not only was she savagely beaten but smoke had been coming off her clothes. When they'd dragged her back to their hideout, they saw the smoke had come from terrible blistered wounds which covered most of her back and legs. She was the first-person Amy had seen who had been touched by the Growth and still lived.

Amy had some first aid experience having been a teacher before the Growth had struck but her limitations meant in the most part their guest's survival was in the hands of fate.

"Is she gonna be ok?"

Amy turned and accepted the tin of Ravioli from her companion. She smiled and ruffled his hair, an action she knew he hated. Amy looked down at the injured woman who's breathing came out in ragged bursts.

"Yeah," she nodded. "I've got a feeling this one's a bit of a fighter."

The Growth LIVES!!

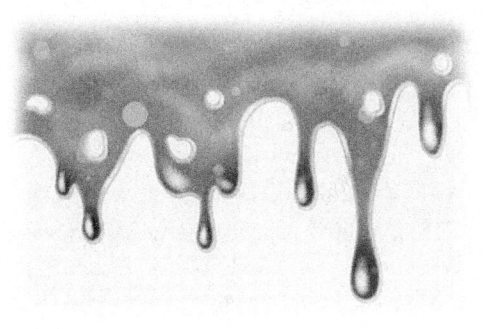

This Is the News

Operation Breakout had seen the successful extraction of surviving armed forces from the U.K. However, the mission had been declared a failure once satellite imagery was analysed from the safety of German headquarters. The terrible progress of the Growth spreading across the North Sea brought gasps from even the most hardened veteran. France was hours away from the same disaster they'd watched befall the United Kingdom and already gridlocked panic and riots followed the populous as they shrunk inland to escape the coast. It was hard to comprehend the creature which still riddled the U.K was stretching to such lengths, and many panicked voices claimed it was only a matter of time before all of Europe would be claimed. What then? Surely the world would fall to the burning ooze and lancing tendrils. The Rattus 11 nerve gas which the British Army had pinned its hopes on was declared a failure and scientists worked around the clock to find something strong enough to permanently push the Growth back.

The Growth

Only the newly promoted Sergeant Wilson knew of the disastrous side effects which Rattus 11 would have had on any survivors in his homeland. The crazed violence it would bring out in humans. Wilson woke up screaming on the few nights he managed to sleep. Yet, hysteria was something the army fought off with the same tenacity they wished to direct at the creature which devoured all in its path. So Wilson swallowed it down and sat dumbly in briefings from his superiors. While the scientists worked, the army tried to keep the peace among the populous.

Easy enough now but what about when the Growth shows up?

Every extradited soldier thought the same thing but pushed it aside to keep the memories of their lost family's company.

Tens of thousands of British immigrants slept in German community centres and on church floors. After weeks of negotiations, both Austria and Poland agreed to house ten thousand each. Camps were set up with tents in claimed fields which had to be protected by armed guards. This was to prevent any attacks from the many far-right groups which were less than sympathetic to those escaping a war zone. Many wanted the Growth nuked but the experts who advised those with the capabilities delivered the same facts. Even if the morality of the situation was ignored and the loss of life was deemed

The Growth

acceptable, the odds of success were too low. Worse still, there were many educated voices claiming the radiation might actually feed the Growth and make it even more dangerous than before. Time was running out and those in power scratched their heads and fumbled for an answer.

Then, on April 19th, exactly twenty-four hours after a stilted memorial service for the victims of the Growth, the military servers were hacked for approximately one minute as displays were interrupted with a message. A quick-thinking operator grabbed a pen and paper, and the note was passed up the chain of command with such urgency it was as though they were dealing with a message from Mars. By the time surviving members of the Ministry of Defence sat with their leaders, a shockwave of excitement had reverberated throughout central headquarters. The first line of the message was coordinates which were quickly checked to reveal they belonged to the same facility where Rattus 11 had been developed. Whether it was out in the open, or in the top-secret briefing Sergeant Wilson was dragged into, the message was read out over and over.

I have the solution. Send help.

This Battlefield Is My Church

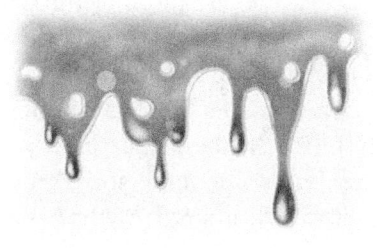

The milk float moved silently down the road and weaved slowly around debris and destruction. A garden chair had its legs welded to the roof of the vehicle and in this makeshift throne sat Michael Applewood who scanned the buildings with great satisfaction. The smell of the dead was a constant thanks to the six corpses tied around the outside of the milk float. Although the leader of the Brotherhood of Change and Growth didn't enjoy being surrounded by such decomposition, he accepted the practicality of their presence. Each rotting body had been subjected to the gas which had been dropped by the bombers in an attempt to destroy the Growth. This was an act of blasphemy as far as Michael and his brothers were concerned. The Growth was doing the lord's work in cleansing society of its sinners. A long overdue reset. Thankfully, the green gas wasn't strong enough to hurt the creature, but it certainly worked at keeping it away. The same couldn't be said for any survivors who'd been caught up in it.

The Growth

Brother George and Brother Alan had got Michael to shelter, and they'd marvelled at the sights presented through the one available window. Plane after plane had roared overhead like in the war movies Michael's father used to force on him. Brother Alan had wanted to investigate but something about the silence which followed bothered Michael so instead they'd stayed in position and observed the green fog rolling across the street like a new beast arriving in town. A man in a torn suit had whirled through the gas, moving like a puppet with cut strings, and the men had watched in fascination as change took hold. The man screamed, cried, and choked his way to the ground. A breeze moved the green cloud, so it momentarily obscured Michael's view. When the suit next came into sight it was upright and the man stared wide-eyed and grinning at the three men who watched through the window. After a moment of tension, the man had screamed and ran headlong so his impact put a ripple of cracks in the glass.

"Get in the cellar," Michael had demanded before the glass gave way.

The three men had spent three days listening to the man smashing every object above them before they ran out of supplies. When they emerged, they were thankful to see the green gas had dissipated, but it had taken all three of them to overcome the fury of the gas induced psychopath. They threw the man's

The Growth

body near one of the many openings where the Growth could be found. The slimy tendrils snaked forward but then quickly retreated back to the hole. It seemed it was smart enough to stay away from poisoned food and a lesson was learnt by all present.

Presently, Michael eyed the death masks of the deterrent which his brothers had strapped to his vehicle. He patted the arms of his chair and smiled smugly.

I feel like the Pope.

Except instead of crowds of adoring followers, the roads were flanked with abandoned cars and ruined buildings. The milk float came to a standstill and Michael thought of Brother Alan and Brother George sitting in the front of the vehicle. Their loyalty made his heart swell, and he couldn't help but blush as he raised the megaphone to his dry lips.

"You can come out now," his voice squawked out along with a touch of feedback.

A breeze overtook them and sent light garbage skyward. Michael smiled at the serenity of the moment as a plastic bag floated up and over the roof of the nearest abandoned building. The sign on the front was still stained green from the gas which had changed desperate people into mindless killers. Once the road fell silent, Michael waited for a few seconds to allow for movement. When none came, he grunted and put his mouth to the megaphone once more.

The Growth

"It would be a lot better for both of you if you came to us. I promise your quality of life would certainly improve."

This brought a snigger from the driving seat but no sounds from the various hiding places the buildings provided.

In the cool shadows of what was once Hargreaves & Sons Plumbing supply, Jason and Tracy stared imploringly at each other. They were a married couple who had only got so far through total acts of cowardice. Their children were long gone because they'd chosen to abandon them, and they were saved from the gas because they just so happened to be in the cellar of a pub, cowering from a gang of looters.

"You can't stay here, it's not safe," the megaphone announced.

Tracy looked at the tired and grubby face of the man squatting beside her and motioned with her head they should go.

"Are you mad?" Jason whispered.

He rubbed his filthy hand over his sore mouth and scratched at his patchy beard. The woman opposite was a stranger to him these days and he had no idea why they stuck together at the expense of every human they encountered. Perhaps it was nothing more than habit and guilt which bound them now. He closed his eyes to the depressing thought and swallowed hard.

"We're here!"

The Growth

Jason stared at his wife in disbelief as she stepped towards the broken door.

"Tracy," he hissed as he missed grabbing her arm by inches.

Michael shielded his eyes to better see the woman come shambling out of the old shop. A man followed reluctantly with his head bowed and the leader of the Brotherhood sized him up as a potential recruit. The woman of course would have to die. Brother Alan crossed the street and motioned for them to follow him back to the milk float. Michael noticed the couple's horror at the vehicle's decoration before turning their eyes up to him.

"Apologies for the gruesome sight but they really do keep our little friend away."

An awkward silence followed as the filthy man eyed Brother Alan's axe which was threaded lazily through his belt.

"Come on you two," Michael beamed. "You can ride up here with me."

"Where are we going?" Tracy asked robotically.

Michael stood from his chair and offered his hand.

"To church, my dear. We're going to church."

*

The only sound was the gentle swish of a stale breeze through the fabric which was

The Growth

fastened to the scaffolding face of the never-to-be finished hotel complex. On exiting the milk float, Jason had marvelled at the "flags" which were in fact nothing more than painted bedsheets. Every phrase read like a threat and Jason knew for sure The Brotherhood Of Change and Growth were going to kill him. Now as he stood at the top of the hotel structure, his eyes moved from the flags to the painted hoods which the men around him wore so obediently. They all smiled at their leader with glazed eyes and Jason couldn't shake the panic which bubbled away in his guts.

They're crazy. Just run. Leave Tracy if this is what she wants. Just get the hell away from these freaks.

Michael smiled serenely at him, and Jason gulped back the paranoia of having his mind read.

"Where are my manners?" Michael exclaimed with a theatrical clap of his hands.

Brother Alan appeared between Jason and his wife holding a jug of water and a plastic cup which was decorated with faded unicorns. Michael nodded and Brother Alan poured the cloudy liquid into the cup before offering it to Tracy. Husband and wife exchanged grim looks. Once the bottled water had become scarce, they had been boiling river water over fires. It was safe to drink in small doses if you could stomach the fact the Growth had probably passed through it. Tracy held the cup up to the sunlight and frowned at its murky contents.

"I'm not thirsty," she murmured through cracked lips.

Now it was Michael's turn to frown.

"What about you, Jason? Are you not thirsty either?"

Jason flinched as Tracy thrust the beaker into his hand. He looked from the expectant faces to the weapons they wore on their belts and then at the dirty water he was being offered. When he looked up to the brotherhood's leader, he saw a familiar look on his face. There was a darkness to Michael's eyes now which betrayed him. Here was a man capable of terrible deeds and atrocious wrongdoing. Jason suddenly brought the cup to his dry lips and tipped the contents into a constricted throat which fought against a heaving stomach.

Don't spit it out for God's sake. You're being tested.

Jason swallowed it all down and gave Michael a weak smile. The darkness immediately left the leader's face and was replaced by a fixed grin which reminded Jason of the vicar his parents dragged him to as a child.

"The Growth blessed that water and now He flows inside you to guide every moment."

Jesus Christ! Jason screamed internally.

The Growth

Tracy whimpered softly and Jason flashed a look of annoyance her way.

Oh, now you're scared.

Jason caught Michael's mouth twist into a slight smirk before the leader continued.

"The Growth is a gift from God, make no mistake about it. All sinners are being purged from the land to make way for a better future. A paradise."

"Paradise?" Tracy murmured almost involuntarily.

Again Michael's face darkened until he regained his composure and flashed a smug smile of contentment at the ragged couple.

"Yes, my dear. Once the chaos has had its say, paradise will overcome, and that is where the righteous will live out their remaining years before ascending to heaven."

Tracy looked at Jason who gave an imploring look to say no more.

Michael clapped his hands together once more and husband and wife jerked as though shot.

"So it is my great pleasure to share with you one of the greatest wonders this universe has ever known."

With that, two of the brothers walked to the edge of the scaffolding and parted two of the flags like curtains. Michael followed and held his arms to the newly revealed sky. He turned and beckoned Jason and Tracy to follow him. The pair walked on jelly legs as the

The Growth

wind whipped through their hair. Michael pointed at a large pit which was around thirty metres from the base of the hotel. Dark shapes moved lazily there. Unmistakably it was the Growth.

"Look at the miracle below."

Jason felt the urge to sit in response to the dizzying height he found himself at. The sight of the creature lurking was the icing on the sickening cake of fear and misery.

"We've been feeding sinners to this gift for some time now," Michael smiled.

"This is your chance for absolution, Jason."

The hooded men seemed to be unnervingly close now and both Jason and Tracy looked around fearfully.

"When we throw sinners from our church walls we get to watch in wonder as the gift emerges from the Pit of Retribution to cleanse the land."

Michael put a hand on Jason's shoulder causing him to flinch once more.

"Would you like to witness such a sacred moment?"

Jason stuttered, unsure of what answer was least likely to spell his demise. Michael smiled warmly and nodded reassurance.

"I'm offering you the chance of redemption, Jason. An opportunity to join our Brotherhood."

Jason felt long tensed muscles relax as

The Growth

he failed to suppress a sigh of relief. Finally there was an option in this nightmare which would mean survival. Jason nodded enthusiastically as though struck dumb.

"Excellent," Michael beamed. "Now, push your wife off the edge."

Jason laughed because he thought he'd misheard. Michael moved to one side so Jason and Tracy could be jostled towards the very edge of the platform.

"You're crazy!" Tracy screamed as she fought against the men who now held her.

"Join us," Michael said calmly without taking his eyes off Jason.

Jason looked back at Michael and thought how easy it would be to grab his wife's wrists and fling her into oblivion. He recalled their wrongdoings since society had fallen. All the cowardly deeds as they had stepped on others, including children, to ensure their own safety. Jason looked at his wife, a stranger now, as she wept uncontrollably.

"Do it," Michael urged him.

Jason looked over to the pit and then back to Tracy. Oh how he had loved her so long ago. It was, however, immeasurable to the hatred which burned inside for getting him into this mess. Despite the mix of emotions and the sheer magnitude of the stakes he surprised himself with his answer.

"I can't," he whimpered.

Without missing a beat, Michael turned

The Growth

to Tracy and smiled.

"Would you throw Jason down if it meant-"

Before the question could be finished, Tracy answered by barging into her husband, so he stumbled clumsily and disappeared over the edge. Jason fell in a confused state, unable to comprehend the level of betrayal. His eyes made no sense of the ground which blurred with his speed, and it sounded as though someone had turned the volume up on the wind as it rushed around him. Jason wanted to form the start of a begging word, but the earth hit him with everything it had. A sound startled him. He was dead before he realised it was his own body exploding.

Tracy's back heaved with the effort and shock of what she'd just done. Half of her left shoe still hung over the edge, so she turned slowly to look at Michael and his followers. The leader held his arms out and whistled in mock appreciation.

"If only Jason had your will to survive."

Tracy smiled nervously and nodded slowly and submissively.

"However, I do wish you'd have let me finish speaking."

Tracy felt the breeze playing with the back of her shirt as her feet and fears teetered on the brink.

"I really hate to be interrupted, you see."

The Growth

Michael began to giggle, and Tracy felt nauseous as smiles spread wide on the hooded men's faces.

"If we were known as the Sisterhood of Growth and Change you may well have stood a chance."

This brought guffaws from some of the men. Michael nodded at Brother Alan.

"Alas, this is a Brotherhood."

Brother Alan took one step forward and planted a big boot into Tracy's chest. Her body landed a few feet from the mess which had been her husband. Dead eyes stared at The Growth which came for them as the Brotherhood watched on from the safety of their church.

Death and Taxes

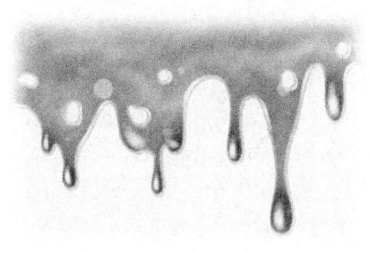

The cell was a cold and timeless place. How long had it been? How many press-ups had been performed? When would they let him leave? Tax had been on the outskirts of a total mental collapse when a new sound reached him. Distant at first but then drawing closer came unfamiliar footsteps. He had grown used to the same guards who rotated shifts to bring him meals and check on him. This was someone different. Someone in a hurry. There was a jangle of keys and then the door opened tentatively to reveal a heavy-set military guard. Tax remained sitting on his bed with his back to the cold wall.

"Stay like that and we won't have any problems."

Tax yawned and watched the guard move out the way so the man in a hurry could get into the small room. Even if he hadn't been wearing full army fatigues, Tax would have known he was a career soldier. His face screamed it to him as did his severe haircut. The man frowned in response to the smell of

The Growth

the room and Tax knew it was because he'd been refusing to shower.

"I'm Sergeant Wilson."

"I don't give a fuck."

Wilson smiled without warmth and adjusted his belt slightly.

"They told me you were a dead loss, and I can see what they mean."

Tax stretched lazily and scratched his short beard.

"Still don't give a fuck, mate."

Wilson laughed quietly and shook his head.

"From what I read, you went berserk onboard the plane, which was saving your arse, right?"

Tax remained silent but the way his jaw clenched gave him away. Wilson, unmoved, continued.

"You put a lot of people in danger and a few of them in hospital because your friend got left behind? They explained afterwards that it was a simple mistake, but you weren't having it were you? You lashed out again and they threw you in here."

Sergeant Wilson raised his eyebrows for a response, but Tax looked away like a petulant child.

"You demanded they turn the plane around and go back to rescue Kevin."

Tax flinched at the name and when he turned to the Sergeant. He had angry tears in

The Growth

his eyes.

"He was my friend!" Tax roared.

The guards shuffled their boots out of sight and Wilson held his hand out to diffuse the situation.

"He's still alive."

Tax opened his mouth wide in shock.

"How? How do you know?"

"He contacted us from the labs in the base you broke into."

Tax self-consciously touched the area where he'd been shot. His mind was racing but only confusion spoke to him.

"How? What about the gas?"

Now it was Wilson who looked uncomfortable.

"He's locked himself away in the facility. The gas didn't take."

"What does that mean?"

"Failed."

"What about the Growth?"

"Still growing."

"You should have listened to him!" Tax flared up once more.

"We're listening now, dammit. That's why I'm here."

"Why?"

"He says he's cracked it."

"Cracked what?"

Sergeant Wilson looked at the big man on the bunk and briefly considered his mental capacity.

The Growth

"The chemical formula to create something to finally destroy this thing."

"Then go and get him then."

"I plan on doing just that, but there's a catch."

Tax stared blankly so Wilson added more information.

"Your friend has specifically asked for you otherwise he isn't going to play ball."

Tax frowned in confusion.

"He's locked behind blast doors and will not come out to us unless you're there because apparently you're the only person he trusts."

Tax watched as the Sergeant's face flushed with anger.

"So it's not enough that I have to lead a small team into a warzone, I've also got to bring some thug of a civilian along for the ride."

"Can you blame him?"

"What?"

"Can you blame Kev for not trusting anyone, when you left him behind?"

Wilson took a quick step towards the bunk and for a split second, Tax thought he was going to be struck.

"Listen to me, you stupid prick. The Growth will hit France by the time we're in the air. Do you understand?"

Tax blinked in response so Wilson continued his rant.

The Growth

"Meanwhile, your friend isn't sharing his information with our science team. He's insisting we go and save him first even if it means tens of thousands more people die in the meantime. If there wasn't a risk of millions dying, then we'd leave him there to rot with his little secrets!"

Wilson composed himself and returned to the wall near the open door.

"You're going to come with me and we're going to get on a plane, ok?"

Tax sat in silence and worried about going back to whatever was left of his homeland. Suddenly the cold cell didn't seem so bad after all.

"Do you want to save your friend or what?"

Tax snapped his head around to look at the military man. The warmth fluttered its return to his gut. It was the same feeling he'd had protecting Kevin on their mission to get to the military. That had ended in failure, but here was a chance to truly make a difference.

"Well?"

*

The aircraft was a lot smaller than Tax had expected and he immediately felt claustrophobic when he took his seat. He realised he was sweating with nerves as they

The Growth

prepared for take-off, so he busied himself with his seatbelt before looking the other passengers over. Sergeant Wilson sat near four soldiers who occasionally gave Tax looks of total disdain. The only man who had been introduced to him was sitting alone at the rear of the plane.

"This is Dipprasad Gurung," Wilson had said. "He's a Gurkha who's been loaned to us."

Tax had found the term strange, but Gurung hadn't seemed bothered by it. Wilson had gone on to tell him that having one Gurkha was like having ten men. Tax turned in his seat to view the diminutive man who appeared to be sleeping and thought Wilson was even more full of shit than he'd first thought. As if on cue, Gurung opened his eyes and stared back with such coldness that Tax snapped his head away and feigned interest in the bag Wilson had given him. The contents were some bottles of water, a blanket, and some rations. Tax looked at the heavily armed soldiers nearby and sighed.

What have you got me into, Kev.

The take-off was even worse than Tax had anticipated and even the boisterous chatter trailed away to silence. From there it was a plane full of nerves which rattled along with the turbulence. It remained that way until they reached the North Sea where The Growth had turned miles of water black. The men listened

The Growth

to Gurung as he repeated the same prayer over and over.

Just Existing

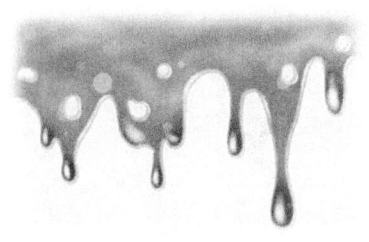

Rattus 11 had stripped people of appetite, thirst, and any sense of morality. The gas had turned them into something wild and primal. Their screams of rage could be heard across the country until eventually their vocal cords gave out and they began to hunt in complete silence. Violence compelled them to wander in search of any remaining survivors who were somehow still hanging on. Over time this new community lost all their hair due to another long-term side effect of the gas, and the sheer amount of walking, combined with a total lack of sustenance, meant their clothes simply fell away. Naked and sinewy, they roamed. These shadows of their former selves were capable of great violence and were known for beating skulls flat and tearing people apart with their bare hands. The only reason supplies were lasting longer was because most people were either dead or forever changed by the gas which had failed to destroy the Growth. They left behind any tinned goods or bottles they'd found and went out in search of the new thing

The Growth

they hungered for.

Amy had been tempted by such prizes and now she was trapped. Worse still, the boy she'd sworn to protect was missing. They'd known of a small gang operating out of a mini market and even caught glimpses of their heavily stocked shelves which they guarded so ferociously. That was before the gas, so Amy's theory was the gang had turned and left all their wares behind. The shop had been empty, and sure enough the shelves had been decorated with months' worth of tinned goods. It had been when Clive had whooped in delight that the sound of rushing feet had erupted on the road outside. There had been no time to think, and Amy had darted through a door which led to stairs. She'd rushed to the flat above which contained nothing, but a mattress-stained brown by a history of violence. Now she sat with her back against the door praying she wouldn't hear the stomping of feet on the stairs. There was the sound of tins clattering to the floor below and the odd glass jar being smashed by the gas affected gang. Amy despaired for the boy and rubbed tears from her raw eyes. It had all happened too fast, but the guilt gnawed at her.

More noises of destruction came from the shop below.

How many? At least two. Maybe more?

She'd heard no screams or cries from the boy, but Amy considered he could still be

The Growth

getting chased down in the street. How easy they would tear his arms from their sockets.

Stop it!

Amy pulled the large kitchen knife from the satchel she wore around her. Exhausted eyes stared blankly at her from the blade's surface, and she tilted it away, unable to accept what she'd become.

There was a thud from below and the sound of rushing feet on the stairs shot up her spine like a jolt of electricity. The door began to shake behind her under the strikes of the visitor who was so desperate to gain entry. Amy stifled a sob and leaned back with all her weight. She hoped the person on the other side would assume the door was simply locked but her heels kept losing purchase on the carpet under the assault on the barrier. Fevered scratching sent shivers across Amy's scalp, and she felt the door open slightly before managing to slam back against it. Amy looked up to see a man's hand trapped there and imagined the mouth forming a soundless cry. Kicks began raining onto the wood and with a shudder Amy knew she had to act before more attackers reacted to the commotion. She thought of the boy, took a deep breath, and rolled away from the door. A heavily wrinkled man stumbled naked into the room and Amy jumped up and attacked without thinking like someone trying to kill an angry wasp. Milky eyes turned to accuse her, but she plunged the knife into the

The Growth

man's neck, so his legs fell from under him. Amy didn't want to let go of the handle, even as blood gushed over her hand, and so fell on the man's spasming body. He thrashed and bucked which caused his wound to gush like a high-pressure sprinkler. Amy rolled away from the soaking and by the time she got to her feet the man's body was still.

Fuelled by adrenaline, Amy paced out of the room and descended halfway down the stairs as quietly as possible. She crouched all the way down to get the angle needed to better see the immediate shop floor. There was no sign of any would-be attackers, but she knew they were nearby. A shelving stack was in the middle of the floor and Amy almost gasped at the sight atop it. Two small feet lay there, and Amy almost wept with relief. Clive was lying on his back out of sight. She descended two more steps and winced at the creaks. Amy could now see a naked figure standing in the shop's entrance. Due to muscle wastage and the fact the figure was facing away from her, Amy couldn't establish whether it was a man or a woman.

Amy knew she had to get Clive's attention and somehow escape, but the latter seemed impossible. Even so, Amy tapped the knife lightly against the nearest wall. She looked for movement but neither the boy nor the person blocking the exit acknowledged hearing anything. Amy gulped and then rapped

The Growth

a salesperson's knock on the wall. A little louder than the first attempt and clearly a noise Clive would understand to be made by someone in full control of their faculties. Sure enough, the boy shakily raised his head to look down his body to the stairs. He smiled bravely at Amy, but it was clear he'd been weeping in silence. Amy held a finger to her lips and Clive returned a look of annoyance as though to say, "I know, I know!"

With a tilt of the head and frantic hand gestures, Amy conveyed she would move to the right of the shelves and help Clive down. The boy was terrified but nodded quickly. Amy inched down the remaining stairs until her boots found the linoleum floor of the shop. She used the stack of shelves to hide her movements from the person in the doorway and took care not to stand on any broken glass. Amy crouched as she made her way around the side of the shelves, wincing as she drew close to the naked form. Her own shadow was cast onto the tins thanks to a large shop window behind her. Clive had rolled onto his side and looked down with imploring eyes.

Amy nodded and smiled to tell him everything was ok. She held out her left hand and jerked her head back to tell him to come down. The boy slowly swung his legs, so he sat upright facing Amy. Clive's eyes looked over Amy's shoulder and suddenly grew engorged with fear. Amy saw the other shadow which

The Growth

had joined her own on the shelves. She turned slowly and saw a hairless woman scream in silence. Amy froze for a moment but then the woman outside smashed into the glass, so cracks raced away in all directions. The person who had blocked the door went to investigate the noise and Amy absentmindedly noted it was a middle-aged man.

"Amy," Clive whimpered.

Amy looked at the boy and then turned back to the window to see the man had noticed them. He looked completely incensed by their presence and seemed torn between helping the woman smash the shop window or rushing back through the open door.

"Clive, get down now."

The boy half fell and was half caught by Amy as there was no longer any point in being quiet. Amy began hammering on the glass with the tip of the blade.

"Run out the door and head back," she demanded over her shoulder.

"What about you?"

"Just get away from here, Clive!"

Amy caught a glimpse of the boy's wounded face. A perfect mix of hurt and anger. Amy's heart sank at the sight but carried on rapping on the window. Clive ran for the door but to Amy's horror the man broke away from the window to intercept him.

"No!"

Amy ran out the door and purposely

collided with the man before he could grab Clive. The boy stopped to look as Amy landed painfully in the road.

"Run!" she screamed as she jumped on the man and began to plunge the knife into his soft back.

"Amy!"

Amy's eyes followed Clive's to see two men had joined the woman at the side of the shop. The knife snapped in the man below Amy just as the three naked forms ran towards her. She knew she couldn't escape and braced for the impact of their murderous intentions. The sound of breaking glass was followed by a whoosh of fire and Amy opened her eyes to flames bursting over her attackers. She turned to see an athletic form throwing another petrol bomb from the other side of the road. This exploded over the legs of the nearest attacker, and he fell, writhing to the ground. The other two attempted to run away but flames licked them hungrily and joined the ones already on the ground. Amy was dragged viciously by her collar to a standing position as the attackers succumbed to the fire. Once released, she turned to look up into Emma's fierce eyes.

"I thought we agreed to stay in our grid?"

Amy suddenly felt exhausted but managed to wave her hand to the heavily stocked shop behind her. She looked like an amateur magician and Emma couldn't help but

The Growth

smirk.

"Please don't do that again, ok?"

"Yes, boss," Amy whispered.

Clive hugged Emma so his head dug into her hip and Amy smiled in appreciation. Emma kissed the boy on the top of his head and hobbled across the road to check the shop out. Amy grimaced at the limp and thought of the battles the warrior woman had endured.

Live Testing

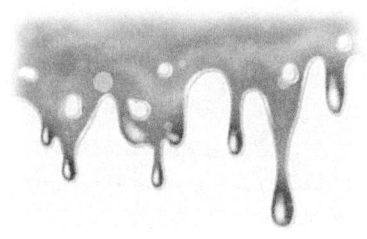

Mercifully, the beard was now long enough to not itch, but Kevin awoke clawing at his chest as though looking for something buried there. Personal hygiene had long since been abandoned and replaced by a punishing routine of running the underground facility alone with the occasional emotional breakdown thrown in for good measure. Wearily he surveyed the sterile lab and pulled the emergency blankets around him in lieu of human contact. Kevin winced against the chair he had slept in and waited for the courage to disengage from its excruciating embrace.

"Come on. Today's the day."

Kevin was talking to himself more than ever before. Since three gas-affected crazies had appeared on his security monitors he had exclaimed today was the day he was going to open the blast doors and deal with them. Now, with his message received by the military, and supplies running low, it really was the actual day. The formula had been ready for weeks but what Kevin had neglected to let the military

The Growth

know was he was yet to test it on the Growth.

"Jesus Christ!" he screamed as he creaked to a standing position.

When Kevin had locked himself away from the gas in a well-stocked and highly sophisticated underground bunker he felt as though he had all the time in the world. For a fleeting time, he'd almost forgotten his troubles. Now though, he felt the clock was suddenly against him. There were expectant people on their way to extract him and he'd promised so very much. Today was the day. The day he would have to fight his way through three violent lunatics before getting close enough to the Growth to use the formula. Kevin shuffled to the monitors and sighed. The three naked forms were still waiting in the corridor directly behind the heavy door and Kevin appraised them with a look of disgust.

"They ignore each other and wander about so they don't seem to be working together."

The tallest of the figures turned quickly to stare straight into the security camera and Kevin recoiled at the man's enraged mouth opening in a muted scream. He closed his eyes and shuddered in revulsion and fear.

"They're not going to leave."

Part of him wanted to wait for extraction and let them deal with the threat outside the door. Then he'd lie about the formula and say it had been tested rigorously.

The Growth

"Coward!"

Kevin kicked a chair, so it clattered along the hard floor. There was an immediate flurry of pounding on the outside of the blast door. For the first time since his visitors had laid siege to his scientific sanctuary, Kevin felt sparks of anger. He quickly began putting on the chemical coverall over his clothes and pulled the hood over his head as though it were armour. Once he had covered his mouth with a heavy-duty mask, Kevin grabbed for the PVC gauntlets. The large trolley rattled as he moved it to the door so it would act as a barricade. Kevin had carefully lined up plastic containers along the surface of the trolley. They each contained a particularly nasty concoction he'd thrown together the day before. He would remove the lids in a moment but first he walked to the nearest clamp stand and unscrewed the parts until he was left holding a two-foot zinc-plated metal pole. The weight was comforting in his hand. Kevin looked at the far end of the lab where two large tables sat at opposite sides of the room. Here the formula was kept in two separate parts to stop it reacting and causing absolute mayhem in his working environment. Kevin knew he couldn't allow the three men to get too far into the lab. He'd have to stop them at the entrance, or everything would be lost.

Kevin put his back against the wall directly to the side of the blast doors. He

The Growth

moved his left hand down to the keypad which hung from exposed wires. The scruffy electronics were a testament to his earlier hacking and rewiring efforts. Pounding on the door grew feverish as though the men sensed the time for battle had finally arrived. Kevin entered his date of birth into the keypad and quickly moved away from the trolley. The deep clunk of heavy locks echoed throughout the complex before giving way to a pneumatic hiss. Carnage was immediate as one of the men collided with the trolley. Kevin watched as the man fell straight over the top of the barricade causing it to fall on its side. The man tried to get up but shivered as though suddenly weakened and began to stare at his hands which sat in a puddle. Kevin knew the mixture was so strong its damage could sometimes be painless, so he was glad to see it was immediately incapacitating the man. He stepped closer to the door and held the metal rod in both hands. The second man entered the room suspiciously eying the other naked man who now lay face down twitching. Kevin swung the rod like a baseball bat from the second man's side, so it connected with a sickening thud. There was a vibration up the pole which Kevin felt through the thick gauntlets. It was the sensation of death reverberating into the killer's fingertips, and it took every ounce of inner strength to keep hold of the weapon.

The Growth

Look at me now, Tax!

Kevin got a glimpse of the caved in face as it fell back through the door into the corridor. He waited for the tall man to lumber into the lab so he could dispatch him in the same way. Seconds ticked by and Kevin wished he could see the security monitor from where he waited. Panic was beginning to rise up in haggard breaths against the safety mask.

Where are you, you son of a bitch?

There was sudden movement to his right and Kevin screamed at the sight of the first man coming for him. His chest and arms were completely ruined by the toxic puddle and the breaths coming from burnt lungs were those of someone who was perilously close to death. Kevin swung the rod, but the blow hit against the man's ribs and slipped from his gloved hands. The metal was ignorantly loud as it clattered to the floor. Instinctively, Kevin kicked out at the man. His boot connected with his attacker's pelvis which caused him to stagger and fall backwards over the trolley. The puddle covered the man's back and he flinched as though electrocuted before finally growing still. Kevin went to retrieve the metal rod but was completely winded by the tall man who sprinted directly into his side. Both men hit the nearest bench and glass smashed all around them.

Kevin was immediately pinned by the bigger man who glared into his face with

The Growth

blinding hatred. Hands ripped at him, and the mask was soon torn away. Kevin marvelled at the small sounds which accompanied these fights to the death. His own grunts met with the shuffling of feet as he found himself staring into the man's gaping mouth. The tall man's hands reached Kevin's throat painfully and they clawed at him. He grabbed the man's wrists and kicked at his legs but to no avail. The tall man seemed to be attempting to tear at Kevin's throat rather than strangle him and the pain encouraged a more robust defence. Kevin stole a glance at the formula lying at the back of the lab before driving his knees into the man's genitals. The reaction from the tall man wasn't the same as it may have been if he hadn't been affected by the gas, but he did release some of his weight from Kevin's aching body. This allowed a desperate reach for a glass beaker which he smashed into the tall man's jaw.

The attack resumed and more pressure clamped onto Kevin's throat as he began to fade out. A glint of light reflected off the shard which protruded from his attacker's throat and Kevin almost lazily reached up and pulled it out. A gush of blood erupted over Kevin's hand and face. The tall man continued his attack but with every jet of gore which he emitted, the force got weaker and weaker. Blind from blood, Kevin was eventually able to throw the man off him. By the time he'd wiped

The Growth

his eyes he could see the tall man lay dead in an enormous pool of crimson. Kevin marvelled at the paper-pale skin and then rushed to the back of his lab. It was time to go outside for the first time in a month.

The exterior cameras had shown empty grounds outside, but Kevin still hesitated in the doorway. First it had been the brightness of day which stopped him in his tracks, now it was the thought of more gas induced killers which held him still. He stepped tentatively outside, expecting the thunder of running murderers to meet him. Between the silence and the fresh air, which felt incredible, he wandered away from the door to the overgrown grass. Kevin turned around in a circle seeing the runway, the fields, and the high fence which had once been enough to keep things secure. A sudden pang of loneliness hit him in the gut, and he felt overcome with the urge to cry. Kevin balled his fists at his side and screamed with tears in his eyes. He roared defiantly in the face of his sadness as a rallying cry. A crow lazily rose from the runway and flew to the nearest tree to better observe this new madman.

"Good morning!" Kevin cried out.

The crow turned away. Kevin carefully adjusted the straps on his bag and thought of the two containers within. They were carefully wrapped in bundled sheets which he had stripped from the beds in the medical wing. Kevin set off walking towards the main gates

The Growth

with the literal expectations of the world on his shoulders.

The farmhouse was only two miles down country roads and Kevin soon saw its roof coming into view. He'd heard nothing but birdsong and felt as though he were the last person alive on Earth. There was a certain thrill to it like the giddying theoretical stories the Twilight Zone had asked of him as a child. Kevin stopped on the stone driveway which led to the farmhouse and listened intently. Once more there was only the sound of birds enjoying a life without mankind. Kevin sniffed and walked to the broken front door. Like many houses he'd encountered in the towns and cities, this one was in a state of violent ruin. The furniture which remained was smashed to pieces and the walls which were still upright were covered with a damp tide mark where the Growth had nearly touched the ceiling. In the centre of the ground floor it looked as though a bomb had been buried in the houses foundations before being set off. A bubble of carpet had burst to reveal snapped floorboards and a hole some twenty feet wide. Kevin looked in to see a mess of broken pipes pulled up through the very earth the house was sat upon. He set his bag down at his feet and retrieved the two large containers.

"Now to get your attention."

Kevin looked around and found a large piece of wood the farmhouse had shed. On returning to the hole he began to bang the broken pipes with the wood while shouting obscenities to the stale air.

"Come on then, you bastard!"

His arms were hurting, and he was stumbling over his words as he started wondering if the Growth could truly be under everything all at once. There was a new sound from below like broken taps suddenly sputtering into life. Kevin dropped the piece of wood and began unwrapping the first container. He glanced into the hole and was disgusted to see the first ooze of the Growth pouring itself out of every crack in the pipes. Kevin worked faster so by the time the hole in the floor was brimming over with the creature he had freed the glass completely. Without hesitation he removed the lid and threw the large jar-like container, so it washed over the dense surface of the Growth. Now all that was left was to keep at a safe distance to throw the second part of the compound, so it agitated with the first. Kevin turned to retrieve the bound jar and saw the large wave of the Growth which had been silently pouring down the staircase behind him. It had already cut off his means of escape and in a panic, Kevin clumsily kicked the second jar, so it rolled away to the far corner of the room.

"Shit, shit, shit!"

The Growth from the hole in the floor was moving rapidly towards him now as

The Growth

though incensed with his earlier bravado while the mass from the stairs was crossing the carpet. Kevin scurried after the fallen jar like a man chasing paper money in the breeze. Wood splintered behind him, and the stink of the thing burned his nostrils and made his eyes water. He scooped up the bound jar, crashing into the wall which marked a dead end.

"Fucking come on," Kevin whimpered as he ripped the binding from the container.

The Growth swelled and joined together until Kevin was completely blocked from the front door. He looked at the small windows styled to make the farmhouse appear like a cottage and internally screamed. The Growth moved slowly, in no great rush to melt him down and absorb his mass. Kevin tried to keep tabs on the area where he'd thrown the first container, but it was becoming increasingly impossible. The Growth was six feet away, so Kevin pulled himself onto the small windowsill. He grabbed at the handle on the window and between his one-handed grip and the one foot he could fit on the ledge he somehow managed to prevent himself from falling to the floor. The Growth bulged as though to show it would soon be able to reach the man in the window. It rolled onto the floor below Kevin and waited for him to fall. His foot nearly obliged, and Kevin found himself shuffling uncomfortably as the handle began bending slightly in his hand.

The Growth

The Growth swelled below forcing him into action. Kevin threw the jar, so it landed roughly where the hole in the floor had been. There was no time to spare as the glass container began disappearing from view, so Kevin grabbed the Glock 17 pistol from his waistband and tensed with all he was worth to stop his body swaying. He squeezed the trigger like he'd been practising back at the base. Bullets hit either side of the jar, absorbed into the Growth, but Kevin kept firing. He was glad of the double-stack magazine the gun favoured and eventually the glass smashed. The second part of the compound sprayed up into the air and rained down. Wherever the two compounds met there was immediate carnage. The Growth grew bubbles which quickly burst as the mass appeared to turn in on itself. Kevin was elated but the handle was going to give and send him to his death at any second.

"Come on!" he roared.

The Growth shrunk in on itself which caused more of the compound to mix. Huge chunks exploded up and Kevin watched mouth open wide as these pieces didn't merge with the rest of The Growth.

It's rejecting the affected parts of its mass!

Kevin suddenly fell from his perch but mercifully the Growth had receded enough that he landed on scorched carpet instead. He instinctively retreated but the mass was too busy dealing with the chemicals which were

The Growth

devouring it in the same way it had done to so many others. After a few minutes it had completely retreated back into the pipes and away from the house. Kevin marvelled at the volume of chunks which had been left behind. Now dead the pieces had the appearance of skin which had been shed by a giant snake. Over half of the Growth which had entered the building had been lost to two jars of his formula. A production line could make heavy dents in the entire creature and given enough time it would be possible to totally eradicate it.

"It bloody worked!"

Kevin laughed with a euphoria he had never before experienced. Redemption for his invention which had once lost him everything and the giddying rush of having just survived certain death. The laugh rattled around the husk of a house until Kevin replaced it with heaving sobs of emotion.

Popcorn

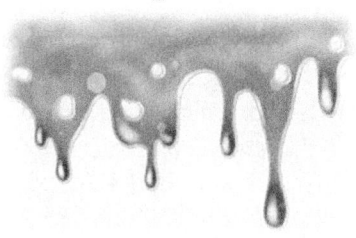

It seemed stupid to bring a kid along on a supply run, yet leaving him behind somehow seemed even more idiotic. Of course, Emma had asked Amy to remain in their hideout with Clive, but then two sets of eyes had stared holes into her.

"Oh I see," Amy had said. "Don't need us now you're back on your feet?"

Emma had given her saviour a friendly pat on the arm which had consequently sent Amy off balance. Presently the three survivors were making slow-going through the ruined high street some two miles from their temporary home. Clive was slowing Amy down and Emma's injuries, which had changed her forever, were a constant reminder of her mortality and failing condition.

"I think we're at the limit of how far out we should go out."

Emma looked back at Amy as she held out a hand to help Clive. The boy frowned in a childish display of independence. Emma smirked at the unlikely duo she had warmed to

The Growth

over the last few months. She couldn't say she'd been the biggest fan of kids before, but Clive was more like a little old man who melted her heart. It amazed her the lengths Amy had gone to keep the boy safe when they weren't even bound by blood. Emma marvelled at the woman, who was too good for this corrupted world, as she ignored what her heart thought about matters. Pangs of guilt made her cringe, so she looked away to the rubble a gas explosion had reduced the nearby buildings to.

"Are you listening?"

Amy was at her side now, huffing from the journey so far.

"Just catching my breath."

Amy snorted out a laugh.

"You? You're like the fittest person I've ever met."

Their eyes caught for a moment and the corners of Amy's mouth twitched slightly. A noise of bricks shifting from the hill of rubble before them snapped them back to reality.

"Come and look at this," Clive called down from above.

The boy stood with his hands on his hips like a proud explorer and both Amy and Emma sniggered as they half crawled, half walked, to join him.

The view was of a cinema which boasted a classic theatre sign. Letters of film titles had been shed so the pavement looked

The Growth

like a chaotic crossword.

"What do you think?"

Emma narrowed her eyes at the smashed front which revealed a ransacked foyer from the early days of the disaster. A popcorn display lay on its side like a relic. Emma recalled laughter and held hands from happier times and took a guilty step away from Amy's proximity.

"I think we should go for it," Clive beamed.

"I wasn't asking you, knucklehead."

Amy and Clive mock wrestled at the top of the ruins while Emma scanned for any wandering threats. They'd been finding more and more discarded supplies lately and the cinema would certainly have been a good place to shelter. Hopefully, there was no one lying in wait for them.

"Ok," Emma finally said. "But I go in alone first to check it out."

Both Amy and Clive saluted before bursting into laughter. Emma couldn't keep the smirk away.

"Wise guys," she retorted as they stumbled down the other side of the debris.

Clive was busy trying to find enough fallen letters to spell out his name when Emma pulled Amy to one side.

"I'm not sure this is the best idea."

"We're here now," Amy shrugged. "Maybe we should all go in together?"

The Growth

Emma looked at the double doors which presumably led to the screens.

"No. You wait here and look after Clive."

Amy held a large knife up to the air in response and Emma nodded her goodbyes. The familiar crunch of glass marked her first tentative steps into the foyer. An acrid smell of burnt electronics met her along with the sights of riotous ruin. A small arcade had been set on fire at some point, so the melted machines were deformed to resemble nightmarish robots from another dimension. The food counter had been ransacked long ago with only smashed glass and splintered wood to show for it. Scorch marks ran up part of the wall to her right where someone had enjoyed a campfire. The fire would have been like a beacon in the darkness and Emma shuddered at the thought of the gas affected psychopaths pouring in like moths to a flame.

Dumb move.

Emma turned and saw both Amy and Clive watching her as though she were the latest movie premiere. The doors creaked unapologetically as she entered a wide corridor which was lying in complete darkness. As the doors swung shut behind her, Emma grabbed the small torch from her back pocket. The scene appeared more like the sleeping quarters of a sunken ship than a modern cinema. Dust floated past the thin beam of the torch like

The Growth

flotsam. Numbers pointed to doors on either side of the corridor, but Emma was fixated on the far wall. The torch wasn't powerful enough to make the journey, so she walked forward on the loud carpet from a lost era. White paint seemingly glowed in the gloom as a symbol began to make sense in the dark. Emma felt her breathing change to make way for the nerves. She already knew what the symbol was but had to be sure. The torch finally found the wall and Emma stopped and gasped at the large sign which was painted there. It was a symbol which was seared into her brain in the same way the Growth's burns were present on her body. The symbol had been painted throughout the hotel complex where she'd nearly lost her life to some damned cult.

Surely, they couldn't have survived the gas and the massacres which followed?

As though in response, there was the sound of metal scraping from the double doors she had entered through. Emma ran to the sound and realised a metal bar had been put through the handles to lock her in. As soon as she began hitting the door with the palm of her right hand, a familiar voice spoke from the foyer.

"You really are a devil woman, aren't you?" Michael Applewood crowed.

Emma froze.

"Maybe even the devil himself."

"You leave them alone!" Emma

The Growth

erupted.

Michael laughed in response and Emma could hear Clive crying somewhere in the background.

"Oh don't worry about these two sinners," Michael sneered. "I'm taking them to church."

"I'll kill you, bastard!"

Michael chuckled again in response.

"I think you'll be too busy for that, Satan."

With that his footsteps began to recede before being drowned out by a nerve jarring racket. Emma couldn't place the loud noise at first as it reassembled nothing more than sonic feedback. However, after a few seconds she realised it was an alarm being played down some sort of speaker or amplifier. Emma didn't have further time to wonder as the door to screen one burst open to reveal a horde of naked flesh seeking her out. The shrill noise was drawing them out and Emma cursed herself for falling into a trap.

*

Michael smirked at the megaphone which lay on the floor. He'd rigged it up with tape to create the constant feedback noise which now drew the crazies out. It was only their presence which was keeping the Growth

The Growth

below the surface for now. Too much noise might be too tempting though, and Michael wasn't about to stick around to find out. He walked back outside where the woman still fought against Brother Alan's embrace. The boy wept openly, while Brother George stood awkwardly at his side as though the show of emotion might bring him to his knees at any moment. Michael waltzed towards the woman in a carefree manner before whipping out the scalpel from his hiding place. Brother Alan switched his arms to grab Amy in a headlock so he could present her face to Michael's blade. Amy froze at somewhere between fear and the strong arms of the man behind her. The scalpel was an inch from her eyeball.

"Either you keep still and allow Brother Alan to bind your hands, or I will take one of your eyes."

Amy was as nauseated with the threat as she was the grin which followed. Michael pointed at the boy with a theatrical flair.

"Then with your remaining eye you can watch as I cut a new smile into his throat."

"Don't you touch him!"

Michael sighed as though dealing with a minor inconvenience.

"I have literally just explained to you what needs to happen to ensure the brat is left alone."

"I'm not a brat!" Clive choked and produced a snot bubble.

The Growth

Brother George responded to Michael's glare by cuffing the boy to the back of the head. Amy sank her teeth into Brother Alan's wrist in response, but the man held firm. Michael swiped deftly and a raw sting exploded across Amy's cheek.

"The next one takes your eye, whore!"

Amy stopped resisting and watched as her face drizzled blood onto the man's hairy arm.

"Just leave him alone," she warned in a quiet voice.

Her hands were bound roughly behind her with rope. She looked up to see Clive suffering the same fate.

"It's going to be ok, mate."

The man behind her chuckled and Amy felt a murderous intent she'd never experienced before. She wanted these men burnt and pulled apart in slow agonising death but knew Clive's life, and probably her own, would be forfeit. Michael gestured towards the awaiting milk float and Amy gagged at the sight of the putrefied corpses which decorated it.

"Let's get away from this terrible noise, shall we?"

There was a sudden commotion from nearby as three naked crazies rushed down the hill of rubble. Michael tutted and nodded at Brother George. The man dutifully pushed Clive towards Brother Alan and walked forward into battle with his cricket bat held out

The Growth

to his side. There was a change in the air when there were only ten metres between the combatants. Amy didn't understand until what sounded like a whip-crack bounced off the walls of the buildings which remained. The head of the nearest crazy to Brother George turned to a red mist and the body immediately fell away. All except the two remaining attackers flinched at the gun report. A second shot rang out and once more a naked body dropped lifelessly to the rubble. Brother Alan began to push Amy and Clive to the milk float as Michael stared in wonder at the unfolding battle. The final naked form rushed to Brother George, but he had shaken off the shock of the gunshots. He timed the swing of his bat to perfection and connected perfectly so that willow wood smashed bone. The clunk sound overtook the noise of the gunshot which was dying away. Brother George stamped onto the gas affected body with vigour until strings of pulp joined the soles of his boot to the dead body. Michael surveyed the nearby roofs but saw no one.

"Seems we have a new saviour, my brothers."

The silence which followed was interrupted by a zipping sound. Brother George's head separated like a water balloon erupting on its target. Michael's eyes widened as he rushed to the milk float. He squashed into the child who yelped at the contact. With four

The Growth

people squeezed into the cabin the vehicle moved off. They all flinched when a bullet tore through the roof behind them. Michael closed his eyes and prayed sixteen miles per hour would be enough to take them out of the sniper's range of vision.

*

Emma heard the gunshots as she collided with the door to screen five. The steady drum of her pursuers on the carpet was constant while she ran towards yet another dead end. Thankfully, there were no more naked forms lurking in the auditorium but the door behind Emma was already crashing open as the mass of killers followed. She made the snap decision to sprint up the aisle to the back wall as a projector watched on unmoved. Clattering came from behind, so Emma made the difficult decision to throw off her rucksack, as her hammer and knife were already threaded through her belt. It was only after she'd lost the bag that a thought occurred to her. Without hesitation she clicked the torch off so the absolute darkness could envelope the entire room. Crashing immediately followed and Emma visualised her crazed pursuers falling over the rows of seats as she pocketed the torch. Running feet darted up the steps and passed by her crouching face by inches. The figure smashed right into the back wall with a thud which attracted those nearest. Emma shrunk back between two rows of seats as the horde beat their hands on the offending wall. With great care, she slowly hurdled one leg over the seat in the direction of the exit. The sound of running feet was all around as they searched for her. Emma couldn't see anything but darkness and fought against emitting any laboured breaths which might give her away. A crash beside her shook the nearest seat and a set of arms grabbed blindly around her waist. Emma clamped her legs to the seat she straddled and stabbed down with the knife towards where a skull pressed into her belly. The blade snapped and Emma hissed against the pain of her wrist bending back. Mercifully, the arms released her so she could continue her slow descent down the slope of seating. Once again, bodies crashed into the rows nearby which forced Emma to change tact. She edged to the furthest point from the aisle until her shoulder hit a wall. From memory, Emma knew the wall angled down to match the slope's descent. She aimed to climb over and drop down on the other side to escape back out of the door she'd entered through. Emma reached one arm up, but the wooden finish was beyond her grasp. She placed the handle of the hammer through her belt and stepped on the back of the nearest seat. Emma leaned into the wall as she boosted herself up. Another collision with the row of seats sent a

The Growth

shockwave up her leg and served as encouragement to hurry. Emma pulled herself up knowing the current height of the drop would mean broken legs. She closed her eyes to the image of raging hands tearing lumps of flesh from her bones. With the grace of a child sliding down a banister, Emma began her escape from screen five. The burning of friction between her denim clad thighs told her she was going to quick, but the darkness ensured it was impossible to get her bearings. She contemplated blindly throwing herself over the side and what the consequences would be. However, before she could weigh up which was the best course of action, the slope ran out and deposited her into the air. Emma fell onto naked bodies which crumpled below her. Thankfully, due to a career of body shots, she was able to roll to her feet without being too winded. With the hammer now back in her hand, Emma darted for the door. It opened onto two figures which she could just about make out in the murky corridor. Emma smashed her hammer into their skulls without hesitation. The noise from the foyer still fractured the air so she flicked her torch back on and headed towards the painted symbol. A fire exit came into view on her left and Emma broke out into fresh air, gasping for breath like someone who'd been underwater for too long. She didn't need to go around the front of the old cinema to know Amy and Clive would be

The Growth

gone. Emma clenched her fists as tight as they'd go and began marching in the direction of the never-to-be-finished hotel.

Battle At Chipperton Airfield

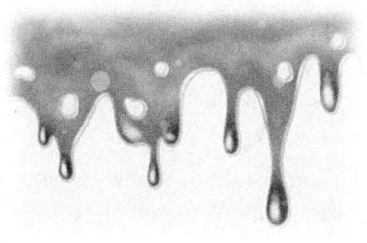

Tax knew something was wrong when Sergeant Wilson returned from the cockpit and immediately buckled himself in. The faces of his soldiers paled slightly, and they followed their superior in securing themselves to their seats. Tax stood and walked towards Wilson. It was a difficult journey as the plane had been banking left for the last ten minutes. Tax grabbed the headrests nearest to him for balance as he walked at an angle more befitting a fairground operator. The Sergeant looked up at him with the weary look of someone who didn't want to be bothered.

"You said we'd be there by now. What's going on?"

"We've been circling the facility for twenty-five minutes, so I was right about that."

The two men stared at each other uncomfortably until Wilson rolled his eyes and broke the silence.

"Look, there's way more debris on the runway than we anticipated, so we can't land here."

The Growth

Tax looked out the nearest window but all he could see was endless sky.

"What are we going to do? We've got to get to Kev."

"There's more to this than your bloody mate!"

Tax was taken aback by the sneer on the Sergeant's face. Wilson rubbed his eyes and sighed.

"There's a small domestic airfield around eight miles from the facility. Hopefully, it's in better shape."

With that, Wilson turned away leaving Tax standing awkwardly and unsure what to do. A heavy-set soldier chuckled from nearby, and Tax fought the urge to give him a slap. He walked back to his seat and buckled himself in just as the plane righted itself and began to descend.

The landing was rough, and Taxs' stomach churned with the hopeless fear of being in the hands of a God whom he didn't believe in. By the time the plane came to a standstill, the passengers were too stunned to speak. Tax let out a deep breath and unbuckled his seat belt. No sooner had it clicked open that loud thudding began filling the silence. Tax assumed the plane was complaining about the boisterous landing until he saw Wilson and his men quickly unpacking their assault rifles.

"What's going on?"

The men ignored Tax and the Sergeant

The Growth

raced past towards the door.

"Garvey with me. Knowles you get the door."

Tax turned and kneeled on his seat to get a better view. The only passenger not moving was the Gurkha who sat with a calmness which Tax found unnerving.

"On three, Knowles."

The soldier nodded and moved to the handle. Tax frowned at the thuds which came from multiple positions now. He looked out of his window and caught a flurry of movement, but the wing obscured his view.

"Three!"

Tax flinched down in response to the immediate gunfire which was aimed through the open door. Short bursts continued as Wilson and Garvey aimed with looks of grim determination. Tax stumbled towards the nearest window and looked towards the open door. His mouth dropped open at the sight of a dozen naked and hairless figures sprinting towards the plane. Precision gunfire cut down the nearest, but it didn't slow the pace of the others.

"Out!" Garvey shouted.

Knowles swapped places with the soldier while he reloaded and immediately began picking off the runners.

"What the fucks going on?" Tax screamed above the carnage.

Gurung gave a shake of his head

The Growth

towards him in acknowledgment.

Wilson brought the final naked figure down with two shots to their chest. A spent shell rattled on the tarmac below and an eerie calm fell over the plane. Tax barged his way to the door to look over Sergeant Wilson's shoulder. Blood leaked from a stack of bodies. They were uniformed in their naked and hairless state. Taxs' head began to fill with questions but only one tumbled out of his dry mouth.

"What's wrong with them?"

Wilson flinched, still keyed-up from the action. For a moment Tax thought the gun would be turned in his direction.

"The gas did this to them," he muttered.

Tax looked from Wilson's haunted face to the human debris, then back to Wilson.

"I don't understand."

"Gas sent them fucking loopy, mate," Knowles said beside him.

Wilson fixed the man with a filthy look which had Knowles looking at his boots before embarking on a tactical retreat.

"The gas didn't kill the Growth, but it did *that* to any survivors."

"Why were they attacking us though?"

"Those things attack on sight. That's all they're capable of now."

"Things?"

"They're not people," Wilson snapped.

The Growth

"Get that out of your thick, skull, right now!"

With that the Sergeant barged past Tax and began barking orders.

"Check your gear and form up a defensive perimeter around the plane until we're ready to move off!"

Tax watched the flurry of movement around him and realised he was equipped with nothing more than a few bottles of water and emergency rations.

"Hughes! Adams! Get out there!" Wilson barked.

The two soldiers bustled past Tax and descended the small steps to the runway. Knowles and Garvey soon followed with heavy packs bouncing behind them.

"You stick with me, Tax," Sergeant Wilson ordered.

"Don't I get a gun?"

"Have you ever used one?"

"No."

"Then it would just be a waste of bullets, wouldn't it?"

Wilson left the plane and Tax looked behind him at Gurung who was adjusting the straps on his pack. He looked like a man who was simply making sure he still had his travelling documents so he could pass quickly through the airport and continue with his holiday. The Gurkha looked up at Tax and nodded at the open door as a reminder it was time to leave.

The Growth

Tax squinted into the drizzle which touched his face like a wet flannel. Wilson was talking in hushed tones with Knowles who stared at a compass and nodded enthusiastically. The other men stood at various points around the aircraft and Gurung ducked under the aircraft to silently assume his own position. Tax was startled by the noise of the steps being pulled back aboard by one of the pilots. The man stared at Tax before shutting himself in to defend their means of escape. Sergeant Wilson approached Tax. He had the body-language of an adult who was about to explain something to a small child. There was no patience in the man's hawkish eyes.

"Listen up, you stay right where I can see you and when I tell you to do something, you do it, ok?"

Tax wanted to punch the man in his throat. He began daydreaming of the soldiers retaliating, his body dancing with every bullet until it fell to the wet tarmac.

"Hey, do you want to save your friend or not?"

Tax blinked the thoughts away and rejoined the conversation. He watched a raindrop run off the Sergeant's nose and down onto his army fatigues. Tax suddenly felt aware he was wearing the same borrowed uniform and felt ridiculous. No gun, no training, no clue. Wilson sensed the man's unease and

The Growth

softened his tone.

"Look, I'll tell you what I know. The gas messed the survivors up and now they're as dangerous as the Growth. They're attracted to noise, and they will kill you without hesitation. Do not think they can be saved because they can't."

Wilson pointed down the small airstrip to a set of buildings.

"The facility where Kevin is waiting is in that direction. We get him, we get back to the plane, and the world is saved. What I need from you is to do exactly what I say and let my team do their job. The chain of command is not in place to hurt your feelings, it's there to make sure we make it out alive. So when I give an order, you follow, ok?"

Tax tried to relax his jaw.

"Ok," he muttered.

With that the Sergeant gathered his men from their formation. Garvey and Knowles picked up point while Adams and Gurung took the rear. Tax walked with Wilson and Hughes through the eerie silence which fell thicker than the rain and with greater persistence. The buildings were closer now and Tax saw most were nothing more than sheds dwarfed by a large hangar. There was a small car park with a few burnt out cars there, but all the planes in the area were gone. Tax imagined the scenes as everyone with a pilot's licence tried to escape the country. The carnage and panic must have been almost unbearable.

Garvey gestured at the hangar and Wilson nodded. Knowles followed Garvey to the giant door while the rest of the team moved low and quickly towards what appeared to be a control station. Wilson and Hughes quickly flanked the next building for signs of life. Tax looked through the windows at the row of empty chairs and the maps on the wall. He assumed he was looking at some sort of training room. Wilson came back into view and motioned to Adams, Gurung, and Hughes to move up and use the side of the building as cover. Tax crouched with the men while they watched Garvey and Knowles getting closer to the large hangar. He gave Wilson a quizzical look.

"There might be a vehicle we can use in there," the Sergeant quietly explained.

Tax looked back down the airstrip. Their plane suddenly seemed far away, as did their escape.

Knowles reached the control unit for the large shutter door. He hoped the power was still active because using the chain to manually open such a large door would be exhausting even for someone with his muscles. Garvey positioned himself on the opposite side to Knowles and gave him a "go for it" nod. Knowles pressed the button and sighed in relief as it clicked into place. The door shuddered and began to slowly open. He took

The Growth

his finger off the button expecting the door to stop ascending but it was stuck in place. Knowles scowled at the noise the shutters were now making. He'd only wanted the door to be open enough so he could crouch under but now there was no stopping it. Garvey took a few steps back and began signalling to Sergeant Wilson. Knowles peered straight into the gloom as the interior of the hangar was revealed. The rainy day only slightly illuminated the shadows, but Knowles gasped at what he could see. Rows and rows of vicious eyes glared at him. Mouths stretched wide in silent screams of rage. Knowles was an excellent fighter. Even when the odds were against him, he would always overcome. He'd once fought off three attackers while drunk outside a pub in Glasgow. Now though, he didn't even have a chance to raise his gun or clench a fist. A wave of dozens of crazed flesh crashed down on his shuddering body. Garvey fired a few shots into the mound which crushed Knowles with a snap of bones. He quickly realised it was time to retreat due to the staggering numbers of the crazed which they'd set free.

"Fuck me!" Adams spluttered at Taxs' side.

They watched as an endless wave poured out of the hangar. Tax thought he was watching the Growth initially before figures broke from the mass to sprint after Garvey. The soldier hefted a grenade towards the

The Growth

entrance which tore limbs from some of his pursuers, but soon at least twenty of the naked forms were chasing him back towards the plane. Gurung joined Wilson, Adams, and Hughes in forming a firing squad which began aiming at those who spilled from the hangar. Tax watched every person who was dropped be replaced by three more. He paced behind the soldiers as he fought the urge to run away. There was a crash from the hangar as another thirty or so attackers clumsily burst from their shelter.

"On me! Go, go, go!" Wilson screamed.

Tax chased after the men as they ran from the scene. Hughes stopped and removed a claymore from his pack and hastily pinned a short tripwire into the ground. Tax looked over his shoulder and saw the countless naked forms closing in.

"Come on!" he screamed at Hughes.

Bullets whizzed by and some of their pursuers fell heavily. Hughes was at Taxs' side when the explosion thudded through the turf below them as the C4 charge scattered steel balls into their enemies. Tax was full of adrenaline but still staggered off course. He didn't look but he heard the human debris rain back down onto the earth behind him. Hughes pulled his sleeve and dragged Tax along to see Wilson and the others flee into a brick building no bigger than an average house.

The Growth

Garvey had always been fast. When he was a kid, he loved to run rather than walk. The thrill of the air whistling past his ears as he pushed his body to new speeds had been a constant which got him all the way to the county sprint team. Now he grimaced against the heavy pack as he brought his knees as high as he could. The slap of a large number of feet on the wet turf behind him was getting closer so he pulled the straps from his shoulders and left the rucksack in his wake. Garvey gripped his gun as he sprinted with all he had. The plane was getting closer but so were his hunters. He remembered the advice his late Grandad had given him before an important sprint meet.

"Keep your eyes straight ahead until you cross the finish line," he'd said.

Garvey found another gear and raced on with tears in his eyes. Once he was fifty metres from the aircraft, he fired a few bullets over his shoulder. Mercifully, the door opened, and both pilots emerged firing careful shots into his chasers. Thirty metres in and Garvey's lungs burned, and his shins ached. More shots whistled over his head, and he imagined naked bodies falling dead.

You can make it, Garvey thought.

The expressions of the men in the plane's doorway betrayed reality and Garvey was grabbed by the shoulder. He was spun to face his attackers and so gripped the trigger

The Growth

down on his gun to feel the vibration rattle up his arm. Garvey was simultaneously struck several times and he whirled around with the dizzying impact. As he fell to the ground, he saw his bullets tear through the guts of one of the pilots and along the plane's fuselage.

Tax and Hughes had just finished barricading the door when the huge explosion rattled the workshop's lone window. Wilson rushed up the steps to the mezzanine floor and looked through the glass. Tax watched the man sag at the view before him.

"What was that?"

"The plane," Gurung told the room without looking.

Shoulders dropped and Tax felt as though the wind had been knocked out of him. The door banged loudly as a reminder of the death which waited outside.

"Now what do we do?" Adams moaned.

Wilson had composed himself and moved down to join them.

"We stick to the plan and get to the facility. From there we'll use our comms to organise extraction."

"How long is that going to take, Sir?" Hughes groaned.

"As long as bloody necessary!"

Wilson looked around at his team and shook his head.

"Pull yourselves together, will you?

The Growth

We're going to fight our way out of this so bloody buck up, will you!"

Tax watched the military programming kick in and the men nodded seriously and checked their weapons.

"Hughes and Adams take out that window and pick off as many of those things as you can."

"Yes, sir."

"And don't blow through all your ammunition!"

The sound of smashing glass made Tax flinch as did the men taking pot shots onto the masses below. Pounding was occurring on all sides of the building and Tax was relieved there was only one door and one window.

"I can throw grenades to the back of the crowd," Adams called down.

Crowd? My God, how many are out there? Tax panicked.

Wilson gathered his grenades and passed them to Hughes on the steps. Adams stuck his arm out of the window and lobbed the first grenade. There was a dull blast and then the sound of soil showering the building. Hughes passed another grenade over to Adams.

"Got a fair few of the bastards," Adams shouted down and returned to shooting.

Tax noticed the pounding moved from the sides and back of the building to the front where all the noise was occurring. If he hadn't witnessed the devastating attack on Knowles, he would have likened the behaviour to lemmings. Hughes had taken over from Adams and shook his head after every burst of his gun as though he were putting down a dog. Tax saw he was crying and looked away.

"My turn," Wilson commanded.

Minutes passed and Tax joined Hughes at the bottom of the steps. He put a hand on the soldier's shoulder who in turn attempted a smile.

"Move the barricade and let Gurung mop up," Wilson shouted down.

"How many?" the Gurkha asked as Hughes and Adams moved a heavy metal table away.

"I haven't got the angle here but there can't be more than five?"

Gurung looked at the door and put his assault rifle down. He pulled out his sidearm and the wide curved blade of his kukri. Tax marvelled at the size of the knife and the expert way the Gurkha held it.

"Ready?" Adams asked from the door.

Gurung nodded and the door was flung open. Two figures fell face first into the room and Adams dispatched them quickly with shots to the back of their skulls. Gurung raised his pistol and shot a third in the face before disappearing out of the door. There were two further shots and then the sound of grunts and

The Growth

shuffling feet. Adams and Hughes followed but no gun fire ensued.

"It's safe for now," Wilson called down to Tax.

They left the workshop together to find Gurung sheathing his blood-soaked kukri. Adams and Hughes were scarecrows in a field of the dead. Tax wretched at the stench of blood and shit while Wilson looked around in wonder. There must have been a hundred corpses between the hangar and the workshop. Minutes passed before the thick black smoke from the airstrip got their attention. A fire raged from the husk of the plane, and it was blackening the grass all around. Wilson checked his compass and cleared his throat.

"Let's move out," he barked.

Bastardised and The Last Sinners

Kevin had seen the plane circling overhead. A day earlier he would have wept with joy. However, the content of the files he'd uncovered had blown everything to pieces. Such was the buoyancy of his mood after the successful field test, Kevin had been ready to share details with the military about the effect of his formula on the Growth. The connection was intermittent so to pass time he'd explored the computer until he landed upon a hidden email folder. The password was bypassed due to the initial tinkering he'd performed to hack into the terminal. With a sinking feeling akin to turbulence, Kevin had read an email chain which broke his heart.

King - I need an update. Client is getting anxious.

Guard - We've got enough of his formula worked out to start testing this week. Will have conclusive results in two weeks.

The Growth

King - I want an answer by Monday or we will lose the contract.

Kevin's heart had raced as he scanned over the next exchange.

Guard - A lot of excitement here. We've got it. It's slower than Gordon's formula but it is leaving no trace of whatever waste we put in front of it.

Kevin had vomited a mouthful of soup to the side of his chair. To see his name in the conversation had shocked him like a taser. They were talking about *his* formula. With a mind racing to piece things together, he'd read on.

King - Excellent. I want you live testing this week.

Guard - Sir, the formula isn't stable enough for us to take it out of the lab.

King - Do you realise how many countries have signed up for this? It's the answer to the world's waste management problems. If they don't see conclusive proof this week then we can forget about being at the very front of this. Do you really think China is going to be far behind us?

Guard - Sir, I understand, but the solution is growing slightly more than projected after every successful

The Growth

test. We'd like to have a handle on that before a real-life trial.

King - I'm not asking! We are dealing with world leaders here and I won't let your team ruin that because you're getting twitchy. Our people are counting on us to come through. Do you know what that means?

Guard - Yes, Sir.

King - I'm going to spell it out anyway so you can bloody well pull yourself together! If we get this contract, then the United Kingdom will be at the top of the whole pile. We will decide the course of the entire world and enjoy the fruits of what comes with that. YOU and your family will enjoy those fruits. However, if we fall at the first bloody hurdle then our people miss out on all of what was promised. You realise they'll be asking who's to blame, don't you?

Guard - I do, Sir.

King - Good. I want footage THIS WEEK which I can wow our clients with. It needs to be clear enough so they believe we can deliver everything we promised we could deliver. Understood?

Guard - Understood. I will begin making arrangements immediately.

The next few messages were threats from whoever King was.

The Growth

King - I NEED THAT VIDEO!

King - Where the hell are you? If you've fucked me on this, then I hope you've hidden your family too!

The tone of the emails changed from anger to worry.

King - Please tell me you're not behind what's all over the news??

King - Is this because of the test, Stephenson? What have you done!?

Kevin had wheeled backwards so the chair clattered noisily to the floor. The date of the last message was the twenty-fifth of May, and it was one he wouldn't soon forget.
"No! Please God, no!" Kevin had yelled.
The pieces collided in his mind, and he collapsed in a heap of misery. Dr Stephenson had been a jealous ex-colleague, and the twenty-fifth of May was the same day the Growth had emerged from the sewers on live television. It was clear they'd bastardised his creation to ensure the right people made their millions. Stephenson and his team had lost control over it though. The Growth had taken on a life of its own hadn't it. No wonder they were keen to listen to him now. Kevin had held

The Growth

his hand over his mouth and grappled with his thoughts. He'd asked for Tax to ensure the man was safe but now it seemed he'd put them both in grave danger.

*

The breeze whipped around Michael Applewood's head, yet it wasn't strong enough to raise his lank strands of hair. He sighed at the loss of Brother George and walked to the edge of the fifth floor. The view below the hotel construction had changed drastically since he'd nearly lost his life there. All the building machinery and equipment had been pulled down and consumed as the pit expanded. Dozens of corpses of the gas induced were piled in the hotel's basement and for now it kept the Growth from sinking the church of The Brotherhood of Change and Growth. Thankfully, the stink of putrefaction didn't reach the heights of his living quarters. Michael smirked at the pit where their saviour waited.

"You wouldn't do that to me though would you?" he whispered.

Michael surveyed the nearest office building which sagged like a concrete husk.

"You've already done so much."

Heavy footsteps pounded the concrete stairs behind him, and Michael smirked. It was another chance to let Brother Alan believe he

The Growth

had eyes in the back of his head.

"Everything ok, Brother Alan?"

Michael waited until the footsteps suddenly stopped and shuffled before he slowly turned around. Brother Alan narrowed his eyes with uncertainty and then blinked rapidly as he remembered he had news to deliver.

"I worry about the girl."

"Why?"

"Some of my brother's look at her in a sinful manner."

Michael clenched his jaw until it produced a dull ache. The ways he fought so hard to eradicate still haunted him like a long shadow he couldn't escape. Perhaps castration would be the way forward, but they lacked the medical equipment to ensure it didn't kill them all. The sooner he could get rid of the sinful bait bewitching his men with lust, the better. She was necessary for now though. Once her friend came running into his trap then he'd have his revenge. His men had spotted her days ago and Michael had rejoiced to the heavens for the opportunity to remove the one stain from his time as leader of the Brotherhood.

"I'll make sure to mention such sin in tomorrow's sermon. Move the woman and boy to the fourth floor and keep guard of them."

Brother Alan nodded with relief.

"I can trust you with that, I assume?"

Brother Alan's face flushed in

The Growth

embarrassment as he retreated noisily down the steps. After a few minutes there was shouting below as he barked warnings to the other men. From the heights of his church Michael Applewood grinned.

They'd grown tired of Amy's screams and gagged her, but it didn't stop her from retching against the rag when the big man grabbed her sleeve to pull her along.

"This way," he ordered.

Clive followed Brother Alan and Amy. He too had his hands bound by rope but wasn't gagged. The child was in shock and there was something about his mournful stare which concerned Amy. It was as though something lay broken and strewn about in there.

He's given up.

Amy was glad to be away from the group of men on the floor below. The hunger in their eyes was unmistakable and thankfully missing from the look the big man gave her. There was nothing lustful there, just total disdain. Brother Alan led them to a cold concrete corner where the only sound was the occasional ripple of tarpaulin in the breeze. Clive sat down cross-legged in a way which suggested he was exhausted. Brother Alan glared at Amy until she followed the boy to the floor. She knelt until her knees grew sore while the big man dragged a plastic chair into place to sit on. Clive sniffled beside her, and Amy wished she could hold him and tell him

The Growth

everything was going to be alright.

"How are our guests settling in, Brother Alan?"

Amy flinched at the voice of the man who approached with a fixed smile on his waxy face. Emma had told her all about the strange man and his cult one rainy night while Clive had been sleeping. She warned Amy they could still be alive. It was hard to believe she was now being held captive while Emma was probably dead. Tears threw Amy's vision out of focus, so she wiped her eyes with one of her bound arms. The leader now stood next to Brother Alan who had jumped to his feet.

"Don't cry, my dear."

Amy swallowed the anger down for Clive's sake, and the man continued.

"I've seen your friend in action, and I have no doubt she lives."

Michael crouched down to be at Amy's level.

"In fact, I'm rather counting on it."

Amy was repulsed with the grin which broke out across the man's face. There was insanity in his eyes, it was as clear as the colouring.

"I am Michael Applewood, welcome to my church. Make no mistake, we do the Lord's work today."

What scared Amy the most was she could tell Michael genuinely believed every word he was saying. She looked at the large

The Growth

man called Brother Alan and was taken aback by the expression on his face. Tears of pride rolled down it and he nodded in agreement with every syllable from his leader's throat.

"You have been saved by the Brotherhood of Change and Growth. We will remove the sin which has blinkered you for so long now. The path you have walked was determined by the devil, but praise God because every single false road has been devastated by the Growth. It is a gift, a saviour, who has allowed for a great reset. Now there is only one path for you, and it is glorious."

Michael wiped spittle from his chin and ignored the whimpers from his audience.

"The Growth was the start. I have been tasked to aid with the finish. My flock will rid this land of the last sinners and we will begin anew. The Growth stripped away all the filth which modern life had become so dependent on. Society was a greedy sow suckling on the devil's teat and God was sick of it. *I* was sick of it! So the Growth was sent down as a wondrous gift. It's a miracle you see? Modern problems were burned away by the ancient and my God how we deserved it."

Michael placed a clammy palm on her shoulder. Amy flinched his hand away and for a moment the anger flashed in his eyes, and she saw exactly what kind of creature he really was. Michael composed himself and leaned close to his captive's ear.

The Growth

"As soon as your whore friend shows up, and she will, you'll get your wings."

Amy recoiled and stared back in horror. Michael straightened up and smiled at Clive.

"You can join us as we watch your friends take flight. Now their path has been corrected, their journey will be one of righteousness."

Amy was incensed by Michael addressing Clive and attempted to wriggle to her feet. Brother Alan cuffed her around the side of her face, and she fell quickly to the cold concrete. Amy watched Michael walk away with a ringing in her ear which was akin to an alarm telling her she was going to die.

Silent Scream

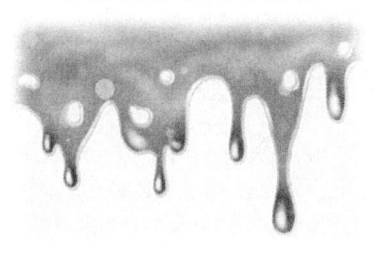

Progress was painfully slow and dangerous. On three separate occasions, Emma had come close to bumbling straight into a pack of the gas induced killers who roamed the city's ruins. It was hard not to rush when images of Amy and Clive sneaked into her mind at every opportunity. Every time Emma had to hide or change direction due to crowds of killers, her imagination conjured images of the cult torturing the two people who had saved her life. To lose anyone else she cared for was unthinkable. The destruction of the cult had been her last wish when she had nothing left, but she'd failed, and the task had nearly killed her. Now though, there were two people stuck right in the middle of the battlefield. A woman and a child being used as bait in a trap made from spite. Emma stooped low and crossed the broken street as quickly as she dared. The ruins were stacked maddingly high behind her, and the only way forward was filled with the noise of rushing footsteps as naked forms searched desperately for prey. Irreparably damaged cars

The Growth

filled the space between them, and Emma crouched to use them as cover. She peered through smashed windows and saw figures passing through here and there. There was no way of telling how many were in the way, but Emma knew her hammer wielding arm would ache and her nerves would be shredded before she made it through. She tilted her head to try and get a better view when a thought occurred to her like an instinct alarm ringing out in her brain. Emma cursed herself for breaking one of the rules of the new world.

Turn around!

The naked form of what was once a middle-aged woman was twelve feet away from Emma's position. She was running silently with arms held high ready to attack and Emma shuddered at the staring eyes and mouth which was open like a large fish feeding. The hammer took the woman's right knee and Emma's last knife worked in and out of stomach and throat. Emma's wrists were coated in gore by the time her would-be attacker stopped thrashing. There was a flurry of movement, but Emma had been expecting it and swung the hammer once more. The blow struck the rushing man in the temple, so he fell dead across the mess Emma had made of the woman. It was an obscene image she had created on the road and Emma had to move away from it before yet more of her mind was captured by madness. She left bloody handprints along the bodywork

The Growth

of the cars she skirted. The heavy pound of feet along the top of nearby vehicles made Emma drop to a sitting position so she wasn't spotted. A stench attacked her nose and Emma gagged against the sensation. It felt as though she had been chewing on spoilt meat. Just ahead she could see the source of the stink. A man was sitting on the road with his back propped up against a van. If all innocence hadn't been filed from her bones, Emma may have thought the man was taking a nap. She winced against the creaking in her knees from moving closer. Emma could see the man's arms appeared impossibly long due to them being stretched from their sockets. His sternum appeared uneven where several people had stamped and jumped on it. The man's face was bloated from death and the savage beating which had been put on it. Emma covered her mouth with the crook of her elbow and blinked against the vapours of nausea which pricked her eyes. She continued her low advance between vehicles, unable to take her eyes from the corpse. Emma shuffled past the bludgeoned man when she noticed the painted hood stuffed behind his neck. Another zealot abandoned by their so-called saviour. Emma spat bitterly on the floor between her and the dead man. Two strong hands grabbed her ankles from underneath the car she was hiding behind. Emma stifled a scream and fell backwards but still the grip on her held firm. She kicked out as her feet

The Growth

disappeared. The hands dragged her inch by inch to a shadowy oblivion. Emma bent to the side as far as she could to hammer at where she felt the hands to be, but it had no effect. The pull was strong enough for her to believe the hands belonged to more than one killer. Inch by inch the shadows pulled her in until her legs were completely underneath the body of the car. Emma sobbed with panic as the pull on her legs grew more painful. Shooting pains rushed up from her knees and she looked at the broken dead man over her shoulder. Emma dropped her weapons so she could put her hands to the car door. She strained against the metal in an attempt to stop herself being scraped underneath to her death. The unmistakable sound of bare feet running on concrete came to her and Emma looked to her side and saw two naked men running to get her. Hands continued to pull, and Emma imagined the crazy popping out of the other side. The running was right near her head when a gunshot shattered the area. Emma saw the nearest runner fall and then another shot rang out. The grip on her released and she heard a wet thud from the opposite side of the car. Emma immediately began crawling back on her elbows to defend herself from the next runner, but she needn't have bothered. A third gunshot cracked, and the man's skull fragments thundered over the nearest car like a brief downpour of hail. Emma retrieved her weapons and squatted against the tyre of the vehicle. Breathlessly, she scanned the nearby buildings for signs of the shooter. Silence fell over the scene only for more running from the direction Emma needed to go. Another two rifle reports echoed down the street and the silence returned.

Who the hell are you?

Emma tried to control the breaths which shuddered from her. She wanted to make a break for it but there were still crazies out there and maybe the next bullet would rip through her back. An image of Amy smiling coyly at her flashed into her mind and Emma found she was moving low down the side of the cars again. A gunshot caused her to flinch, and Emma was certain she'd been shot until another dead crazy fell into sight a few cars ahead. The skill of the shooter was immaculate, and it gave Emma confidence to keep moving.

If they wanted me dead, I'd already be face down in the road.

Emma snaked around various abandoned vehicles. It seemed a bullet would fly by whenever one of the gas-affected marauders came into view. Not a single shot missed and eventually Emma found herself at the end of the bottleneck which the timeless traffic jam had presented. There were no more killers nearby, so she stood up to better scan the surrounding area. The sun had broken the clouds and Emma used a bloodied hand to

The Growth

shield her eyes. A silence had fallen but she knew the shooter was still out there watching her. Emma was about to give up searching and turn away when a sound rang out down the street. Somebody was purposely tapping metal on metal and when Emma followed the noise, she found a figure standing on the roof of a ruined shop. From such a distance, and with the sun in her eyes, it was impossible to make anything out from the silhouette. Emma couldn't even tell the gender of the sniper. She waved like a child on a bus to complete strangers and couldn't help but smile when the figure slowly waved back. Eventually, Emma turned in the direction her journey required with the hope her guardian angel would follow and thin the numbers of the cult once she arrived at her destination.

à Aimer et Perdu

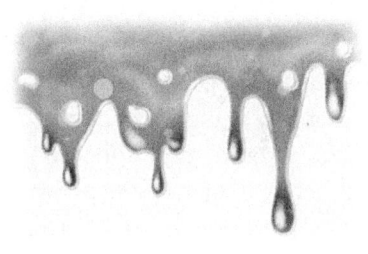

While the people of Le Havre fled east like a cloud of disturbed flies, Jean had somehow managed to coax his battered Citroen south so it could shudder down the A29. Le Poudreux had been a gridlocked hellscape as roads were throttled by sheer weight of numbers. Jean had felt like a salmon exerting all his energy to make it upstream. The roads were a tide of cars and in this case the hungry bears waiting on the banks were the military barking at him to turn around and head inland. Jean had given up on making Honfleur and instead zig-zagged across country with one fearful eye on the rapidly depleting fuel gauge. He'd made it as far as Touques on fumes before his car slowed to a halt. A considerable walk remained but Jean wouldn't be deterred. His late wife Isabelle had often smirked and called him a "selfish old man" and she had been right.

"I am very selfish, my love," he'd grunted and grabbed the urn from the passenger seat.

Now though, he felt as though his

The Growth

selfishness was going to kill him with exhaustion. Jean's throat was constricted with a thirst which felt like a rusty nail lay there. He didn't care to think about his blistered feet but comforted himself with the fact he'd never have to take his shoes off again. The streets were now deserted and even the military had packed up and headed inland. Weapons were useless against the Growth so were used to police the people instead. Jean watched litter swish past and thought it might be best if people stayed away altogether from now on. The hotel where they'd enjoyed a wonderful honeymoon was nearby, but Jean couldn't bring himself to visit. Deauville beach was his destination and finally it was in sight.

"Nearly there," he told the urn tucked under his arm like a rugby ball.

Anarchic sounds from a nearby side street hurried him to sea and soon he stood awkwardly on the sand. Deauville beach where he'd proposed to Isabelle a literal lifetime ago. She had always loved their weekends away and even though Jean had hated the sand he was quick to get down on one knee in its grains. For surely that was what love was all about?

Love is sacrifice, Jean thought.

The salt air stung his eyes and Jean felt warm tears worm their way down his gaunt cheeks.

"You're crying," the urn told him.
"It's the breeze."

The Growth

"Always making excuses," the urn chuckled.

Jean wiped away tears and joined in with laughter of his own. How many times had they laughed bitterly together after the diagnosis? Jean looked left and right as though crossing a busy road. The beach was deserted, and he was glad of it. Hotels rose up behind him, but he ignored them as he walked the white sands to get to the sea.

Jean stood up to his knees in the waves and winced at the immediate pain in his feet. The tide felt different from anything he'd experienced before, and he knew the Growth was closing in.

"I don't want to let you go."

"A promise is a promise!" the urn scolded him.

Jean nodded sadly and gently unscrewed the top. A thousand romantic statements collided with empty religious babble as he turned the urn upside down. Jean watched his wife take to the strong northern wind and collide indiscriminately with waves and sand. Isabelle was one with her favourite place, which in the end, was all she'd wanted.

Jean let go of the empty urn, screwed up his fists, and screamed at the horizon. The release was dizzying, and he had to open his eyes wide to stop himself from falling over. Jean noticed the darkening of the sea now. Like a giant oil slick the Growth grew closer and

The Growth

closer to where he stood. Jean thought of the cancer which had robbed his wife of everything as it committed its hostile takeover of her insides. He saw the same beast out in the waters now and spat in its direction. The way in which the Growth had feasted upon the UK was reminiscence of how the disease had fed upon his wife's ability to perform the most simple of tasks.

"I hate you!"

Jean's voice was lost to the gusts from the sea. Defeated, he closed his eyes and sobbed. The Growth pressed forward, swelled by the tons of sustenance it had found in the crossing. When Jean opened his eyes, he saw the sea was an unusual colour. Fifty metres away the darkness of the Growth could be seen stretching for mile after maddening mile and the water which immediately surrounded him was discoloured by the sediment its journey had wrought. Soon those waters would be occupied by the Growth too.

I'm ready, Jean thought.

He'd wanted to die since his Isabelle had become bedridden and now it seemed long overdue. Jean listened to his ragged breath leave his lungs. It sounded fearful and he cursed his cowardice.

The noise of a dog barking excitedly disturbed the stand-off and Jean whipped his head over his shoulder with a scowl etched there. A mongrel paced back and forth a couple

The Growth

of metres from the water. A bitch with exposed ribs which screamed she was a stray.

"What do you want?"

The dog hesitated, tilted her head, and then began barking again.

"Get the hell out of here!"

The dog came closer to Jean so the last of the normal water licked her paws. Jean threw his arms in the animals direction to scare her off. The dog cowered and Jean felt a pang of guilt.

"I'm sorry, girl but you've got to go."

His voice sounded strange to him. Jean had been talking to himself for the last six months, but it had always been a cynical thing with blind anger coursing through it. For the first time in so long, his words were touched with care and compassion.

"Please get off the beach."

The dog came closer, and Jean held out his old hand. For a moment, the dog's nose sniffed ever closer but then she backtracked away from the water. Jean took a step to follow as though allowing the dog to befriend him was the most important thing in the world. Suddenly he stopped with the presence of the Growth burning somewhere behind him.

"Very clever," he smirked at the canine.

The dog barked as though telling Jean off.

"No, you get off the beach. I'm

The Growth

staying."

The dog growled at Jean, who in turn lost his temper.

"This is my end not yours. You have no right!"

Once again, the dog edged into the water and Jean lowered his hand as fresh tears streaked his face. The dog snuffled his wet hand and began licking his fingers. Jean could hear bubbling from behind him now. He didn't want the dog to die. Jean would have to live to save the persistent animal and so for the first time in a year, he wanted to survive.

"Come on, girl," he cried as cheerfully as he could.

The dog trotted at Jean's side as he tried to jog away from the sea. A combination of age, sand, and wet trousers caused him to stumble, and Jean shot a fearful glance at the bubbling waves. The Growth erupted out of the waters like lava and rushed across the wet beach to meet him.

"Go!" he screamed at the dog.

Jean staggered on aching legs over mounds of sand. When he looked to his side the dog was gone. Barking from behind stopped him in time to see the dog was shouting at the evil which stretched all the way from the coast of England. Jean felt the burn in his lungs as he ran back for the dog and scooped her up when the Growth was nearly upon her paws. Through gritted teeth he ran

The Growth

with everything he had left. The sound of his panting was rivalled by the sizzling of sand behind him. Jean looked at the dog which had replaced the urn under his arm and shook his head at the foolishness of life. They were nearly at the treeline which gave the hotel swimming pools a sense of privacy. Jean hoped they, and the wall which followed, would give him enough time to catch his breath before completing his escape. Suddenly, the sand rushed up to his face with only the impact telling Jean he'd fallen. A deep fatigue overwhelmed him, and he decided his journey was at an end. He'd fulfilled his final promise to Isabelle and saved the dog. Enough was enough. The sizzling became a fury of heat and Jean braced himself for impact. Instead his arm was tugged by the snarling snout of an incredibly determined animal. Sand fell from Jean's stubble as his eyes met his saviours. He shook his head and heaved himself up so he could run once more. The dog had learned the odds now and raced ahead through the trees and stopped at a wall which came to Jean's waist. He heaved the dog over and quickly followed to the sound of collapsing trees. They ran down the side of the abandoned swimming pool and across a redundant tennis court. Jean ran with everything he had while the Growth followed slowly with a distressing inevitability. For now though, six legs searched for a means of escape. Jean and his dog were heading east

The Growth

to join the rest of France who wanted to live.

Muck and Bullets

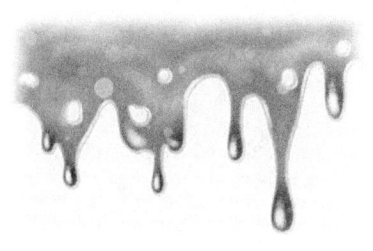

The men looked haunted. Tax noticed a wild look in their eyes which hadn't been there during the flight. He was still shaken from the events at the airfield and the loss of four men, and he assumed the survivors suffered the same way. However, after a slow mile, Tax realised it was the devastation the Growth had wrought which had humbled the team into silence. He'd just assumed everyone had still been in the country when the Growth tore through. It never occurred to him some of the men may have already been overseas. Gurung had taken to scouting ahead and occasionally reporting back to Sergeant Wilson. Most of the time he got within a few metres of the group before anyone noticed him, such was the skill with which he moved. Each time the Gurkha conveyed hushed updates, the Sergeant's face grew slack with stress. Hard enough making it to the military facility while bypassing all rivers and canals without having to navigate through the wreckage as well.

"I used to live five miles from here,"

The Growth

Adams muttered in Taxs' direction.

Tax looked around at the streets which resembled Berlin after the second world war.

"I'm from up north."

Adams stopped walking to contemplate this, eyed Tax with something close to pity, and then walked away. Tax clenched his jaw in response.

"Fucking toff."

Up ahead was a rise in the road and Gurung suddenly held a fist aloft. Wilson gestured for Tax to follow him into a crouched position. Gurung began to motion wildly before rushing out of view.

"Get off the road," Wilson hissed.

Hughes and Adams darted behind a mountain of bricks, the jingle of their packs a new constant in Taxs' life. Sergeant Wilson motioned for Tax to follow him and led him to a partially collapsed building. Once inside he took up position near the splintered doorway to better observe the road. Tax wheeled around in an attempt to understand what the building had been before the Growth had destroyed it. The task was made impossible by a past fire which had cooked the room at some point. Blackened walls had removed any evidence of their function. Tax viewed the melted pile of plastic in the corner of the room with trepidation. There was something else within the debris, something charred and crooked. Flashbacks from the last time he was home

The Growth

forced Tax to look away.

Wilson looked down the sights of his SA80A2, turned away with a grimace, and then returned to the scope. Tax crunched over glass and ashes as he worked his way behind the Sergeant. The view was a gut-punch. Over the hill came the naked victims of the desolate city. Mothers, fathers, sisters, and brothers of the apocalypse wandered the road. Those who'd survived the early massacre the Growth had thrown at the country were now nothing more than ghouls. Tax felt his eyes sting at the sight, but before he moved away, Wilson offered him his sidearm.

"Flick that to take the safety off and just squeeze."

Tax accepted the Glock 17 with a knot in his stomach. He'd thought a firearm would make him feel safer, but he just felt burdened with responsibility. The Sergeant fixed him with a firm look.

"If those things breach this room, then I suggest you put that thing in your mouth."

Tax swallowed dryly and was still thinking of eating a bullet when the first gunshots rang out from the other side of the street.

Adams and Hughes engaged the horde with rapid fire which tore through skin and bone. Tax watched in horror as the people swarmed in the direction of the bullets. Although many fell, the tide was getting closer

The Growth

and closer to the soldiers position. Wilson raised his gun again but didn't take a shot. Tax watched the man screw his eyes shut and lower the weapon. The gas riddled survivors continued to pour forward as the gunfire became more sporadic. Wilson turned and gave Tax a grim look.

"Come on."

Tax followed the Sergeant expecting him to rush towards the hill with his finger on the trigger, but Wilson sneaked back the way they'd come from and disappeared up the side of the building. Tax stumbled over debris the building had coughed up with a sense the Sergeant would leave him behind if he didn't catch up. Wilson looped around so they now faced the way they needed to go. They jogged parallel with the road which they could no longer see due to the wreckage of the street. A shrill scream from where Adams and Hughes had been positioned rang out and caused Tax and Wilson to freeze. More gunfire began accompanied by a battle cry until it too was abruptly cut off. Wilson began running now and Tax did not hesitate to follow the man as he dodged around stacks of bricks and long dead fires.

They used the buildings as cover as they moved up the hill. Tax felt certain he could hear frantic footfall on the road as the crowds sought them out. After a further ten minutes of scrambling unseen, the men

The Growth

stopped behind an upturned lorry.

"We should have helped them."

"Don't give me that shit," Wilson seethed.

"We didn't even try."

"How long from when we left the building until they screamed?"

Tax thought for a moment.

"Less than a minute?"

The Sergeant nodded with eyes bristling with rage.

"So you know we didn't have enough time to save them. I could have taken six, maybe seven before having to reload. There were at least sixty of those things back there!"

"I'm just saying we should have tried."

"You can't even shoot," Wilson erupted. "You know what, give me that back."

Wilson snatched the gun from Taxs' hand and returned it to his belt. Before Tax could complain, the Sergeant began moving forward once more.

They made it another mile before being forced to stop by a giant fracture in the land. Tax sneaked a look into the sinkhole-like crater. The Growth lay there like rainwater in a pothole. Tax backed away quietly and shuddered at how it just waited. Wilson scanned for a way around without having to double-back, but it seemed hopeless. Movement came from the crater and the men took a few more steps backwards. Tax waited

The Growth

for a tendril to snake over the edge in search of them, but none came. There were more sounds of movement, but they were fainter now, so Tax decided to chance a look. He was surprised to see the crater was almost empty with the last of the Growth slowly disappearing up a large waste pipe.

"It's leaving," Tax whispered to Wilson.

The men exchanged confused looks before a noise caused them to look back down the road. The horde had finished with Adams and Hughes and were now running their way. The gas affected masses explained the Growth's disappearance and Wilson jumped into the crater without a second thought. Tax felt it crazy to dive headfirst into an area where the creature had just been, but the sight of the ghoulish mob was enough to send him flying after the Sergeant. The area facing them resembled an extreme climbing wall and Wilson immediately lost his footing and slid back to the bottom as Tax bolted past. Wilson watched as the stocky man used his momentum to launch himself up the vertical part of the climb and grab a large piece of concrete. Tax began kicking manically into the compacted earth to make footholds. The bowl Wilson stood in obscured the view back down the road, but he could hear the rushing of frenzied feet getting dangerously close. He looked up at the dead end before him and

The Growth

prayed his training and guile would be enough to get high enough to escape hands which would want to pummel him to death. Wilson gave a nervous glance into the pipe which the Growth had escaped down before dashing out of the blocks like a sprinter. Tax had made no progress and looked down from his position fifteen feet up the wall of debris. He watched the Sergeant hurtle up the slope of the crater and jump at the wall which he held onto. Wilson winded himself as he collided with the mud and his hands flailed for something to hold onto. Gravity won and the Sergeant rolled painfully to the exact spot he'd set off running from.

"Fuck!" he screamed as he jumped back to his feet.

Tax carefully turned his head a little more so he could see the road behind them. A crowd of ghouls hurtled towards them in unnerving silence. Mouths wide but no sound. They were so close to the crater that Tax knew the sergeant only had one last chance to scale the wall before the mob collided with him like a wave of bludgeoning agony.

"You've got this!"

"Shut up!" Wilson spat out before lunging forward.

The sergeant kept his head down and pumped his legs as quickly as he could manage. He surged up the slope with his gun tapping him on his back like a reminder of the stakes.

The Growth

Wilson took one last great stride like a long jumper and propelled his awkward frame up the wall where he grabbed hold of the bent rebar, he'd been eying up. Tax was to his right and a few feet higher, but he hadn't found a way to further his ascent. The sound of soil flying came from below and the Sergeant winced at the sight of the naked mob flinging themselves into the crater. Tax watched too as the area below was quickly filled with a writing mass of bodies with eyes staring wildly back at them. Wilson tried to advance up the wall, but his boot slipped and for a moment he had to hang by one arm until he corrected his position.

"Stuck," Tax groaned.

Wilson ignored the man and looked across the wall for a means of escape. After realising Tax was the only object in reach, Wilson looked down at the certain death below. All heads were upturned to look at the two men hanging from the wall.

The bastards are just waiting for us to get tired and fall.

Even now he could feel the tendons stretch in his arms as gravity pulled at his boots. Wilson glanced at Tax who was pale and looked like someone who couldn't hold on for much longer. The Sergeant was wishing for a grenade when a rattle of gunfire interrupted the perverse standoff. Tax watched in disgust as the naked forms climbed over each other to

The Growth

chase down whoever was shooting at them. The crater emptied save for a few stragglers and Wilson let his aching hands release the rebar. He controlled his slide as best as possible and brought his gun around on its strap to drop the remaining ghouls before they had a chance to attack him.

"Who's shooting?"

Wilson looked up at the soles of Taxs' boots.

"Gurung, I'd imagine. Now come down while he's bought us time to escape."

*

Gurung ran from the horde, not through fear, but to run them into his trap. He'd swapped his pack for another automatic weapon near the fallen bodies of Adams and Hughes. The weight was making it difficult to stay out of reach from the crowd who chased him down. Gurung had felt nothing as he'd looked down at the mutilated soldiers. A coldness had replaced his heart after losing so many of his brothers who he'd shared a base with back in Darlington. He'd volunteered for the mission so he could die in the country where so many had fallen. Now though, Gurung ran in a trance-like state of someone closing in on the end. So many inspirational acts of sacrifice and bravery were the foundations of his regiment, and he hoped his

The Growth

brothers were looking down on him with approval. The guns looked like extensions of his arms as he ran off the road into an overgrown area. Gurung knew the murderous ghouls behind would follow, in fact he counted on it. The two buildings came into sight, and he jumped over his trap before arriving in the narrow gap between the two high walls. Gurung moved back slightly but remained visible to the pack to resume his role as bait. Pale figures collided with each other in their haste to reach him. The quickest broke through the tripwire so the white-hot shrapnel of three grenades tore through them and those nearby. Gurung raised one of the SA80's, tucked it under his arm, and fired steadily into the thin ribbons of smoke. Once the clip was empty, he dropped the weapon, and held the remaining SA80 in both hands to take advantage of the grip and improve his accuracy. The mortally injured front runners were pushed aside so more ghouls could rush towards him. Gurung expertly dispatched them with short bursts from the gun. With each pull of the trigger he retreated two steps. Once the smell of petrol began to sting his eyes, Gurung turned and ran to his next position. He fumbled in his pockets as the thump of feet echoed between the two buildings behind him. Finally, Gurung produced his father's lighter and ran to the petrol-soaked rag he'd left nearby on his first way through the area. A figure emerged from

The Growth

the gap which forced Gurung to raise his gun again. Two shots to the chest sent it reeling so Gurung could set light to the rag. The flame nearly licked his hand, so he threw it to the slick patch nearby. A petrol can had been an unremarkable find in a country where vehicles were largely redundant, but Gurung smirked as the flames snaked towards the gap in the buildings. He moved back into view to see a dozen or so figures dance in the fire to an agonised song of heat and pain.

Now they really came for him. Some still on fire, some with waves of smoke trailing behind, all with the same cruel look on their gnarled faces. The ground behind Gurung raised up so it sloped above the buildings he stood near. He fired five more rounds before sprinting away from those who wished to destroy him. His mind told him to stop against the burn in his throat and the aches in his legs. Gurung pretended it was the voice of his late father.

Stop running. You've done enough.

Gurung clenched his teeth and shook his head in response.

You saved those men. They're sure to have gotten away by now, my son.

Gurung responded to his own mind by digging into the hill with his heels to try and climb with more speed. The grass was longer, and it made a swish sound against his pants with every step. He didn't bother to turn.

The Growth

Gurung knew they lurched after him with murder on their gas-addled minds.

The men will find the cure. The Growth will be destroyed, and your brothers avenged. That's not your fight now. Your fight is here. Stop and face your death.

Gurung stubbornly headed for the summit. He could hear the grass being trampled over the noise of his own laboured breathing.

Go out fighting, Dipprasad. You are a hero, my boy.

Gurung staggered onto the top of the hill and quickly turned to face his attackers. The sight took his breath away. His gunfire had alerted more of the gas-affected berserkers, and he watched as they poured up the hill from all directions. Gurung thought of the ants nests he would disturb as a child. Now they came for him. He lifted his gun and began picking off those closest. Naked forms dropped rapidly and fell into the legs of those behind, which in turn caused a human traffic jam. They crawled over their dead relentlessly, but Gurung blasted them away too. Between the higher ground and his shooting, it felt for a moment as though he may actually be able to repel them all. Then a familiar click told him all bullets were spent. Gurung threw the gun away and adjusted his beret. He smiled weakly at the clouds which watched him impassively.

Sit down. Rest. You've done enough, son.

Gurung looked out at the ruins of a lost

The Growth

society and drew his Kukri from its sheath. The low sun glanced off the machete like a universal gesture of approval.

"Ayo Gorkhali!" Gurung screamed.

Their hands came for him but were swiftly amputated. Blood sprayed across the trampled grass and over Gurung until he looked like a demon who'd decided to perform his own sacrifices. They swarmed around him, and he felt blows connecting with his back and head. Gurung spun and swung the blade, but his arm ached with exertion. He ducked under a vicious blow and swiped so the machete disembowelled the attacker. Something jumped on his back and Gurung fell to the wet battleground. He managed to wriggle free and get to his feet, but his weapon was lost.

Enough! Your Kukri has been satisfied.

Gurung roared defiance at the masses and sidestepped around their quickest. He pushed one over and ran to a large stone which he noticed jutting out of the ground. Gurung kicked at it and hefted it in his hands. With dull thuds he struck two more in their temples, so they fell to the ground. He tried for a third but lost his balance through exhaustion. Kicks and punches rained down on him the second he fell atop an attacker. Ribs broke and he was blinded in one eye by a long-nailed finger. Still Gurung fought. For every second the masses wasted killing him, was a second for the Wilson and Tax to escape the area. Then the Growth

The Growth

would be destroyed, and his brothers would have justice. This was his small part to play, and he gritted his teeth to the pain of it. Gurung's left arm was pulled from its socket and he wept as multiple sets of hands broke it like a branch. He felt the black edges creep to the corners of his remaining vision. His right hand snaked into his trouser pocket as his collarbone shattered. Gurung allowed reality to fade away and for a moment he felt weightless like the sombre clouds. His mind showed him an image of his dying body at the top of the hill as dozens more crazies rushed up the slope. Gurung smiled at the carnage through bloodied teeth and pulled the pin from the grenade he'd hidden in his pocket.

The Twelfth Round

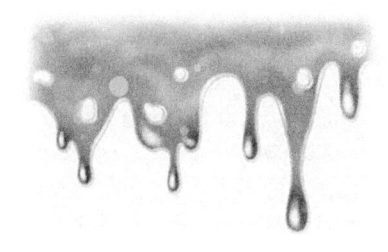

The abandoned hotel resembled a haunted house rather than a church and Emma grimaced at the sight. Banners flapped in the breeze and Emma glared at the nonsensical symbols which had been painted there. She seethed at these "righteous men" who hid behind the Growth's shadow. All her life men had looked down on her. The abuse she got during her boxing career was nothing more than excess fuel to a journey propelled by anger, born from years of derogatory bullshit. Emma stood across the road from where they held Amy and Clive and hefted her hammer, so it rested on her lean shoulder. She scanned the areas between the banners for any signs of movement, but Michael Applewood and his followers were well hidden. Emma felt sick at the thought Amy and Clive could already be dead. She prayed the cult still needed them as bait and took a few tentative steps forward. As she got closer, Emma realised the ground directly to the front of the hotel was occupied by the Growth. The brotherhood were using it

The Growth

as a moat and Emma gagged at the stink of it. She looked around frantically for a way into the building and saw a wooden walkway. It came out of a smashed in window on the second floor of a nearby shop and snaked up to the third floor of the hotel. Emma squinted as she appraised the condition of the bridge. It looked like a strong breeze would bring the whole thing down onto the Growth below.

Emma was about to move to the shop to gain access to the walkway when a whistle rang out from the front of the hotel. Once more, Emma scanned the open areas of the building until finally she saw a figure waving at her. It was unmistakably Michael Applewood and Emma was sure she could feel his smugness even from such a distance. She pointed her hammer at the man and moved for the shop when a scream stopped her in her tracks. Emma looked up to see another familiar figure thrown from near where Michael stood watching her. It was unmistakably Amy, and Emma watched as her friend fell, flapping like a flightless bird, to the Growth below. Emma dropped to her knees at the grotesque sound of impact. Amy's screams were abruptly cut off and Emma screwed up her eyes tight.

Once again, she had been unable to save a loved one's life and something inside her broke like the mechanism of an ancient clock. Emma couldn't breathe. Her body shuddered with a tide of grief which wanted to jump out

The Growth

like vomit. A strangled sob escaped her throat, but the fire of rage burned there and boiled any tears. With eyes bulging a scream erupted from Emma which she turned into a long cry of fury to help purge her soul of all the hurt. Some of Michael's men shuffled uncomfortably at a sound so fierce and primal. Even their leader lost his grin. Emma jumped up and wiped her face on the back of her sleeve. She ran for the shop because once again there was only one purpose left; to rid the world of these disgusting men.

Emma was through the door before realising rushing into the shop was the mistake, they'd wanted her to make. She was grabbed from behind in a bearhug by the man who had been hiding behind the door. Another rushed forward holding a length of old rope. Emma's arms were pinned but she was heartened by the fact the men were trying to capture her rather than kill her. If they had intended, her dead she'd already be bleeding out on the dusty floor of the dilapidated shop. Galvanised by the shock of life's frailty, Emma leaned back into the man who held her and brought both of her boots up and kicked out at the man with the rope. The impact hit him under the jaw and closed his mouth like a door slamming shut. His head rocked back and when it returned to look at Emma, rotten teeth dripped from his mouth on strings of blood and spittle. The man staggered away trying to hold his teeth in and

The Growth

the bearhug slackened at the sight of it. Emma wriggled with all her strength to free her arms before her captor could compose himself. She drove the hammer at his kneecap with all her might. It sounded like a mallet hitting a tent peg and he roared with the sickening pain of it. The second strike sent him to the floor. Without hesitation, Emma towered over the man and brought the hammer down onto his skull.

Robotically, like someone working in an abattoir, she then walked to the second man. He was too preoccupied with the agony from his destroyed mouth to notice, so Emma drove the claw of the hammer into the back of his skull. The man sighed and fell lifeless to the dust. A door led to the stairwell, and it flew open as another hooded figure ran in. He stopped abruptly and stared at the chunk of scalp which hung from the bloodied claw. Emma registered the flicker of fear in the man's eyes and ran to it.

Michael eyed the shop anxiously. His men were taking too long, and a knot was forming in his gut. He nodded at Brother Joseph who tapped Brothers Simon and Phil on their shoulders. The three men hustled down the stairs until Michael saw them arrive at the hotel side of the walkway. Brother Simon placed a tentative foot on the wooden bridge and eyed the smashed in window opposite. Emma appeared and slowly climbed outside to face them. She looked like a corpse which had

The Growth

been jet-washed with blood. The only sign of life was the bright eyes which stared back and the teeth which sneered at the men. Brother Simon felt a shove in his back and glared at Brother Joseph before stepping out towards the bloodied figure. Emma knew their numbers sought to wear her stamina down, but the bridge would only allow them to come for her one at a time. She rolled her aching shoulder and moved onto the walkway. Her half of the bridge hung over the road, whereas the Growth waited below the half which fed into the hotel.

"Get rid of her," Michael shouted from above.

Brother Simon moved forward with a purpose and Emma noticed the thin knife in his hand. The rules of engagement had changed suddenly like the breeze, and she steeled herself to it. Emma felt the bridge flex under their steps. She looked down at the timber which had been nailed in as reinforcement. Although Emma was confident it could bear the weight of a couple of adults, she wasn't confident of being able to fight successfully upon it. The closer the opponents got to the middle of the bridge the more it flexed. Brother Simon felt a giddy sensation and took a nervous glance below. He saw a pile of bricks from a destroyed wall which had once acted as a partition between the road and the hotel development. Suddenly the bricks were

The Growth

rushing towards him before he could understand what had happened. Emma remained lying face down on the walkway where she had thrown her weight the moment the man had looked over the side. She watched him cartwheel through the air before bursting on the rubble below. Tendrils grabbed the remains and pulled them out of view.

Brother Joseph and Brother Phil exchanged nervous looks before the latter moved out high above the Growth. Emma got to her feet and clenched her hand around the hammers handle. The man approaching her was much taller and she worried about his reach. Emma also knew he would be wise to her trick which had disposed of the first man. She watched as he edged closer and closer to her. Emma stayed rooted to the spot and waited for her moment. Brother Phil was two metres away when Emma threw her hammer. His reflex action was to throw up his arms and jerk his head away. The metal painfully collided with his forearm and Brother Phil realised he'd made a fatal error. Emma was already upon him when he lowered his arms, and her shoulder barge sent him screaming over the side. Both Emma and Brother Joseph watched the man slide into the ooze which bubbled fiercely and stripped the flesh from his bones in a matter of seconds.

Michael had seen enough and ordered Brothers David, Neil, and Paul into action.

The Growth

Only he and Brother Alan remained with the child. Emma huffed in exhaustion as Brother Joseph stepped onto the bridge. There was a commotion from behind the man and Emma's heart sank as three more hooded men joined him. Brother Joseph grinned at Emma who raised her hands in a guard to show she was ready and able to continue fighting.

"Time to die, bitch," the man shouted.

Emma screamed psychotically in defiance and the man visibly flinched. She took a shaky step forward when a gunshot rang out. Brother Paul's jaw hit Brother Neil in the face. All looked at the dead man and then hysteria took over. Brother David made a break for the hotel stairs, but a bullet tore straight through his spine. Emma watched in shock as Brother Neil ran for the bridge.

"No, don't!" Brother Joseph shrieked.

Emma lay flat once more, but this time hugged the wood with all her strength. Brother Neil's panicked run onto the walkway shook it violently to the side causing both he and Brother Joseph to step out onto fresh air. Emma closed her eyes to their screams and the exertion of holding onto the bridge as it tilted rapidly from side to side. For a moment it felt as though it were going to completely tip her off but with a bang it righted itself and Emma pressed her forehead into the wood in total relief. It was a feeling which quickly turned to guilt as she recalled Amy's smile. Rejuvenated

The Growth

by anger and the snipers help, Emma marched across the walkway until she arrived at the hotel's stairwell.

Michael pulled the scalpel from the inside of his robe and carefully removed the plastic lid. One look at Brother Alan had the large man hauling the child up by his scrawny wrist. Michael had watched his plan fall apart with every brother who had fallen from the bridge or been blasted by the unseen gun. Even now, he hid with his back to a large concrete pillar as Brother Alan dragged the boy to the edge of the balcony. Michael seethed at his luck.

Have I not been tested enough, Lord?

Michael bowed his head in shame at having questioned his saviour. Then it came to him, and he looked toward the stairwell with a smile spreading larger and larger over his greasy face.

"One last test," he called to Brother Alan.

The big man was busy shaking the boy so he would stop writhing against his grip.

"Put him down!" Emma cried from the top step.

Michael curled his lip in disgust at the woman he regarded as an agent of Satan. Gore was clumped in the creases of her clothes and in her hair, while blood had sprayed across her face. Michael stared at the eyes which shimmered back at him.

The Growth

"I'd choose my words more carefully if I were you."

Emma took a step towards them which evoked a chastising tutting noise from the head of the Brotherhood. Brother Alan hefted Clive up to indicate he would throw him over the edge.

"Get off me," the boy cried.

The murderous purpose which had propelled Emma up the stairwell was leaking out of her in streams of doubt, and so she stopped advancing towards the men. Images of her dead lover as well as Amy falling from the hotel jarred her like pinpricks to her mind. Michael jabbed his blade in her direction.

"Finally we meet again," he grinned. "I'm not sure how you survived your last visit here, but I can guarantee this is the end for you, whore."

The word stung Emma into action.

"What is it you're basing the whore label on?"

"Look at you!"

Michael's face was crimson, and spittle gathered in the corners of his mouth. Emma saw just how far the man had mentally slipped.

"Oh, you mean because I'm a woman?"

Michael struggled to find the right words so Emma continued before he could interrupt.

"Let me guess," she smirked. "Silly

The Growth

little man hates women because they don't like his limp dick?"

Michael's face changed as though someone had slapped him.

"You dare come here with your blasphemy after sending my righteous brothers to their deaths."

"Righteous?"

"Yes, righteous and good men!"

"Who helped you kill innocent people."

"They were sinners! Every. Single. One."

Emma shook her head quickly.

"You're mad."

Michael sneered before nodding at Brother Alan who grunted and hefted Clive higher. Emma was frozen to the spot in fear she would lose the child as well as his guardian. She noticed the big man was trying to keep the bulk of his body hidden behind the concrete structure so only Clive was exposed to the sniper's view. Every scenario of attack she could think of resulted in her death and the demise of the child she was trying to rescue.

From across the road a well-trained eye stared down the power scope of a Heckler and Koch PSG-1. Emma and Michael flinched at the blast from the rifle. Powder-like blood shot from Brother Alan's wrist, and Clive fell to his feet. The boy tried to scurry away as the huge man howled in agony. Emma noticed Michael

The Growth

rushing to Clive and ran to intercept. Michael reached out for the child but was pushed backwards by Emma as she rushed in.

"Get out of here," she cried out to Clive.

Emma felt brief relief as the boy headed for the stairwell. Then a strong hand grabbed the bottom of her leg, and she looked down to see Brother Alan staring up at her with wild eyes. Fire broke out across her face and Emma looked up in shock to see Michael had slashed her across the cheek with his blade. The unhinged man swiped again but this time, Emma weaved backwards so the scalpel swished an inch from her nose. The counterpunch was devastating, and Michael staggered away with a broken nose. Emma looked down at Brother Alan who was still preventing her from walking. She looked at his right arm which hung uselessly at his side and noticed the hand was only partially attached to the wrist. The wound was frothing gore onto the concrete. Emma adjusted her stance and brought her free leg up so she could stamp down onto the injury. Brother Arthur roared as Emma's heel crunched his finger bones. The shock and pain were so much it caused his reflexes to take over and he ripped his arm away from her boot. A jet of blood flew across the nearest wall as though someone was being careless with a painting job. Brother Alan squealed at the stump which his wrist now

The Growth

tapered to. Emma looked down and kicked the severed hand away like a piece of trash. The huge man knelt down and blubbered at his injury. A shadow crossed his face which caught his attention enough to realise a hammer was being brought down between his eyes.

Michael moved his hand from his face and winced at the sight of thick blood and mucus. He turned to see his most loyal disciple lying in a puddle of his own making. Brother Alan's left boot twitched from the last sparks of a dead brain. Michael caught movement through the haze of tears, but the hammer smashed his right kneecap before he could move out of the way.

"Get here, fucker," Emma seethed and lifted the man by his greasy hair.

Michael raised the scalpel, but his hand was viciously twisted back until he dropped it. Emma began dragging Michael towards the balcony's edge with the cult leader resisting at every step.

"Please stop!"

"Like you stopped for Amy?"

"Who?"

Emma was incensed the man didn't even know her name. That he valued human life with such disdain made Emma clench her jaw so tightly it felt as though her teeth would crack. Her response was to smash the hammer into Michael's face. She heard an unusual pop as his eye socket fractured. The man's legs gave

The Growth

way and Emma was able to get him in a headlock and drag him the rest of the way without duress. Once the cold breeze hit them, Michael began to panic. His feet couldn't get purchase on the ground due to the spill of blood Brother Alan had put there. Emma pushed Michael so he whirled around and teetered on the brink of falling. His arms flapped pathetically as he fought desperately to regain his balance.

"I am a prophet. I have been reborn as an angel!" Michael pleaded over his shoulder.

"Then fucking fly!" Emma screamed.

She kicked out at Michael and connected with his back. The founder of the Brother of Change and Growth emitted a high-pitched scream and voided his bowels as he fell through the air. His wide eyes took in the sight of the creature which had waited so patiently for him.

Spare me, he thought.

Michael collided with the jelly-like membrane and felt a flash of white-hot pain as the fat and muscle fall from his bones.

Emma watched every second of it before looking out to the roof opposite. A man in a police snipers uniform stood as though waiting for her appraisal. He had the body language of someone returning from a war, exhausted and haunted. Emma held a bloodied hand up and the man waved back in return before slowly turning away.

The Growth

"Wait!" Emma shouted into the breeze.

It was no use. The man had moved out of sight once more.

Emma found Clive waiting for her near the makeshift bridge.

"Are you ok?" she asked him.

"She's gone, isn't she?"

Emma nearly choked on the lump in her throat.

"Yeah. I'm sorry, mate."

Clive sniffled and nervously wiped his eyes. Emma fought tears of her own and lowered herself to one knee so she could be at the child's level. Everything hurt with the movement, and she wondered if it was worth carrying on now, she'd erased the cult from existence. Clive looked at her expectantly and for a moment Emma felt a deep uncertainty. Then she reached out and ruffled Clive's hair like Amy used to do. The boy squirmed and chuckled as he remembered the sensation he used to complain about.

"Do you want to get out of here?"

Clive nodded enthusiastically.

"Come on. Let's leave this city." Emma said as she held out her hand.

Feels Pretty Personal to Me

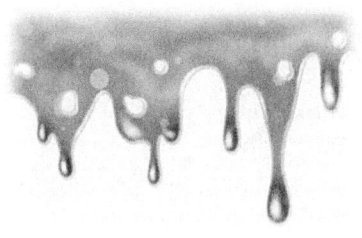

The men were filthy and exhausted by the time they reached the chain link perimeter of the military facility. Tax felt the strange sensation of someone arriving back to a place they thought they'd never return to. It was an unsettling feeling which was heightened by being so close to the part of the fence he'd been straddling when a soldier had shot him from a hidden position. Tax touched the area where he knew the scar shimmered and stared ruefully at the top of the nearby barricade.

"What's up?"

Tax looked across to Wilson who was checking his handgun. The last of the automatic ammunition had been spent two miles earlier, and the Sergeant had tossed the weapon away like a spent water bottle. He held the handgun up and eyed Tax so suspiciously that the latter felt compelled to answer truthfully.

"I got shot near here."

Wilson nodded as though mulling over a friend's weather prediction.

The Growth

"Let's move to the gate."

Tax watched Wilson march away and realised he would gladly take another bullet if he could walk with Kevin instead of a jumped-up military man.

The gate was bent so badly out of shape that a small vehicle would have been able to pass through. Tax thought of the naked ghouls who had killed the rest of his party and suddenly felt worried for his friend. They walked towards the main building in silence as the sergeant pointed his gun at any blind spots. The journey had made them twitchy and once more Tax was amazed, he was still alive. The facility where he'd nearly died from a gunshot wound was looming over them like an unkempt giant. Filthy windows and guttering which resembled wild gardens greeted them.

"He'll be in the underground lab."

Tax looked at Wilson and nodded dumbly. He felt a sudden nervousness in his stomach and had to think about it. Tax realised after a few beats it was a feeling of guilt which gnawed at him. Would Kevin hold a grudge about being left behind? Tax was glad he'd have a chance to explain things soon.

"Come on. He won't come out unless you're with me."

The sergeant bristled with resentment and stalked around the side of the building. Tax followed and cast a glance at the cracked runway they'd been unable to land on. When

The Growth

he looked back, Wilson had disappeared. Tax froze in place until Wilson's head and shoulders emerged from the top of the steps which overgrown weeds had partially hidden.

"Keep up, for Christ's sake."

Chastised, Tax rushed to the steps. Wilson took point after retrieving a thin torch from his pocket. Tax sucked in a breath as the beam washed over a set of bare legs lying on the floor. Wilson moved the torch slowly to reveal the corpse of a gas affected man. The light moved down the short corridor until it reached a heavy door. Wilson nodded at Tax in a way which suggested they'd reached their destination. The Sergeant relaxed his shoulders and stepped over the corpse. Tax flinched at the sound the door made when Wilson banged his fist against it.

"It's Sergeant Wilson. Open the door."

Tax moved to Wilson's side as they listened to the pregnant silence ringing in their ears. The sergeant raised his gun as though he were about to use the grip to knock on the door again. A muffled voice came from behind the door.

"What?" Wilson demanded.

"Wait a minute!"

Tax couldn't help grinning at hearing Kevin's voice. The sergeant looked at him with complete disdain. Mercifully, the door heaved open.

"Hello, Tax."

The Growth

Tax appraised Kevin and was shocked by his friend's appearance. The length of the man's hair and beard were to be expected but his gaunt face and hawkish eyes were a disturbing precursor to starvation. His friend had not been looking after himself. Kevin flashed a sad smile at Tax as though he knew just how badly he looked.

"Alright, Kev. It's good to see you."

The men were about to embrace when Wilson barged past Kevin to get through the doors. Tax followed the sergeant until all three men stood in the laboratory. The room smelt strongly of urine and Tax cast a worried look at his friend. Suddenly he felt as though the cell he'd been living in wasn't so bad after all.

"So, here's your precious friend," Wilson gestured at Tax.

Kevin nodded and smiled at Tax.

"Now is the time to give me the formula."

"The data is ready to send," Kevin said with a point to the one functioning terminal.

Tax looked at the sergeant and felt cold at the sudden change in the man's body language. As a man who'd been surrounded by danger even before the emergence of the Growth, Tax recognised trouble. Wilson's feet were planted, and his jaw flexed as he kept clenching his teeth. Tax dashed towards the sergeant, but Wilson was already lifting his handgun. The deafening gunshot rang out as

The Growth

Tax collided with Wilson so they both smashed through a trolly and onto the floor. Tax began raining punches down before Wilson could protect himself. When the soldier grabbed his arm, Tax adjusted and drove his forearm and elbow into the man's face. The grip loosened to the sound of broken cartilage, but Tax continued to strike into Wilson's face like a baker working with dough. He'd known. Somehow, he'd always known he'd have to kill the soldier.

"I think he's dead, Tax."

Shocked out of his rage, Tax turned and saw Kevin lying on his back while grinning through bloodied teeth. Tax jumped up and ran to his friend so he could cradle his head. Both men looked down at the oozing wound in Kevin's chest.

"What's going on? I don't understand," Tax sobbed.

"I knew you'd get him, Tax."

Kevin grabbed Taxs' hand and although the latter was scared with how cold it was, he gripped it tightly.

"Why? Why did he shoot you?"

Kevin coughed and Tax heard the bubbles there. For a while it seemed like his friend wouldn't be able to provide an answer but finally the cough subsided.

"They messed with my formula and produced the Growth."

Tax was equally stunned and confused.

The Growth

"The army made the Growth?"

Kevin coughed and sucked a gulp of air through gritted teeth.

"Powerful people in the government. They fucked it up and lost control. It changed and kept growing."

Tax looked across at the pulp which remained of Wilson's face.

"I asked them to bring you because I wanted to know you was ok," Kevin continued. "Then I found files. Files which told me everything."

Kevin went still and Tax shook him.

"Stay with me."

"Sorry, mate," Kevin whispered.

"Why are you sorry, you dickhead?"

Another cough wracked through Kevin's ruined lungs as they flooded. He eventually righted himself and looked up at Tax with a fresh look of steely resolve.

"I wouldn't have asked for you if I knew they were coming to kill me."

Taxs' head was spinning.

"Why do they want you dead? It's not your fault, it's theirs!"

"Because I was too close to it. Too close to all their secrets. They left me behind because they must have thought I was more of a threat than a solution."

"Ok, just rest yeah?"

Kevin shook his head rapidly. His face was a grey colour which Tax wouldn't have believed possible unless he'd witnessed it.

"It's too late for me, but you can still be a hero, Tax."

"No. What do you mean?"

"I need you to send the data."

"I can't do it! I'm not smart like you!"

"I've written it all down over there. You can read, can't you mate?"

"Yeah, just slowly y'know."

"Good. That's good."

Kevin whimpered and then coughed violently. Tax closed his eyes to the tears just as Kevin grunted a chuckle out.

"When you send the data it will show the world how to destroy the Growth. It will also send the sordid details of how the Growth came to be. Names and all."

"I'm gonna get those bastards." Tax muttered bitterly.

"We'll get them, Tax. *We'll* get them."

Tax looked into Kevin's glistening eyes and waited for more information before realising his friend had died in his arms.

*

Tax didn't have a clue of the chain of events he'd started through Kevin's instructions. Nor did he know of the repercussions for those responsible. He'd been too busy building a funeral pyre for his friend. Tax had considered burying Kevin but the

The Growth

thought of the body potentially being dug up by something turned his stomach. The way Tax saw it was that warriors came in all different shapes, sizes, and abilities. Kevin had pushed through personal terror and cowardice to try and save the world, so he definitely deserved a warriors cremation in Taxs' eyes. They had both learnt so much from each other. A coward forced to fight, and a brute forced to think. Tax smiled dreamily at the thought. The flames crackled and the smoke stung his eyes which were already sore from crying. Tax turned away to escape the pain and noticed two figures walking slowly across the abandoned runway. He moved around the fire to get a better look. One was unmistakably a child, and as the pair got closer, a huge grin broke out across Taxs' face.

"It's Emma bloody Holt!"

Emma smiled and raised her arm in a weary wave of recognition.

"Didn't think I'd see you again, Champ," Tax beamed as he walked out to the pair.

"Same," Emma smiled.

"You alright, lad?"

Clive scrunched up his face at the ogre-like man before him. Emma gave him a nudge.

"I'm fine, thanks."

There was an awkward silence before Tax noticed Emma trying to get a better view of what was on the fire.

The Growth

"Your friend?"

Tax swallowed hard to words which wouldn't come. He nodded once and then clapped his hands together rather than let fresh tears fall.

"Right, I'll show you inside so you can get some rest."

Emma and Clive followed Tax into the shadows of the large building.

"Any food?" Emma asked.

"Oh yeah. I found a whole store of it in the other building."

Clive stopped suddenly and eyed the building with fear and suspicion.

"Is it safe?"

Tax lowered himself so his eyes were at the same level as the child's.

"You're safe with us, mate," he smiled. "I promise."

Clive surprised Tax by holding out his hand, which he dutifully accepted. Then the boy grabbed at Emma's, so he was flanked by both adults. As they walked closer, Emma admired how easy the building would be to defend from any of the crazies who might wander out to the countryside. Once inside the shelter, she saw stains on the floor where bodies had been dragged away. Tax explained what Kevin had achieved as best as he understood. Emma hadn't been surprised it was a man-made problem but gasped at the potential for the Growth to be wiped out. It

The Growth

seemed incredible that there might be a chance at a new life when she had lost so much of her old one. That night, Clive slept soundly for the first time in weeks, but Emma and Tax tossed and turned while wondering what kind of world would rise from the ashes of such evil greed.

*

    Kevin's note had enabled Tax to send the information to all corners of the world. He had no idea the data had reached every military and scientific system which still functioned. The chemical was branded a miracle and was mass produced on a scale not seen since the last world war. As long as the activator was kept separate from the rest of the formula, it could be transported wherever it was needed. Countless bombing runs were performed over the North Sea and the coast of France. Some planes dropped open barrels of the formula while others carried a payload consisting only of the activator. The result saw substantial portions of the Growth annihilated. However, some smaller pieces spread down towards the Mediterranean. Although many more would lose their lives to the burning mass, a vital foothold was now held by the world's remaining military might.
    Of course, the more affluent countries were slow to help those in economic crisis until

The Growth

there was public outcry regarding the needless death toll data which poured across the twenty-four-hour news networks. Finally an end was in sight as teams were deployed to wherever the Growth could be found. Specialist task forces were formed to deal with the threat using their new weapon which were now at the spearhead of chemical warfare. Those in charge projected dealing with the Growth would one day be as insignificant as calling for pest control to exterminate a rat. Expatriates pressured for a return to the United Kingdom, but their leaders stalled due to unsettling satellite imagery which showed crowds of gas affected killers still roamed their lands. For now they urged caution and didn't believe it possible for any ordinary person to survive there. They had no idea of the extraordinary people who were doing just that.

Pandemic Lessons

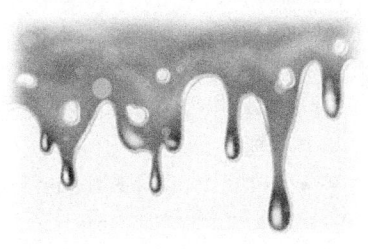

It's interesting, and hopefully not too self-indulgent, to write a little about my experiences of writing The Growth duology. As I sit in the same chair from where I originally wrote both books it is difficult not to get a little nostalgic. I am of course getting a little ahead of myself so let's go back to 2021. A publisher asked me to write another creature series due to working with them to release a debut creature-feature trilogy. Without sounding ungrateful, by that time the elation of being published had eroded into a jaded sense of being boxed in. The first two books of the trilogy had been conceived as a novel which I wrote to stave off depression during the lockdown procedures of 2020. I was assured by the publisher that to release it as two novellas was what readers were clamouring for and so followed their advice. It was during the writing of my third and final novella for that contract when I realised selling a series to readers is extremely difficult. So obviously I was a little sceptical when the same publisher asked me to write another creature-feature series. However, after a positive video call, I agreed. Important to note I had learnt some lessons by only agreeing to sign on for two novellas this time, but I concede I was still brand new and a little naive to the writing and publishing world.

I was sent away to think of a new creature and get cracking. It quickly became apparent that my mind had moved on from the creature-feature format of the Cursed trilogy and I began to panic. I wanted to write about working-class life, and I wanted to write about the failings of our governments. Now I was in a contract for two novellas, so those ideas seemed very, very far away. I work full-time and I have two young daughters who rightfully need my attention so I can't quickly write my way out of situations. Then it hit me. What if my creature was pushed into the background? What if it was part of the landscape/environment rather than hogging the limelight? I realised this would allow me to write the kind of characters, suffering the right kind of narrative I was itching to construct.

Tax stalked onto the page as my enforcer. I wanted an unlikely hero and this man who had been used time and time again for his brawn struck me in the heart. He was the kind of guy I pass in my "rough" town every week. I wanted the honesty of what living in this environment can do to a man and I'm happy with how Tax turned out. Through

The Growth

reader feedback I can confirm he is certainly one of my most popular characters. I think it's because of how vulnerable such a strong man can be when impacted by mental health issues. There's also Taxs' desire to help people at all costs which lends him a purity that we all find both compelling and sincere. I wanted to write about a man pushed to the brink and forced into daily retaliation. A man who becomes a vigilante for the right reasons. I think I achieved that, and Tax showed us he is truly "the inevitable man."

Kevin was constructed more in line with the science aspect of the narrative. Perhaps not quite as "likeable" as Tax, Kevin is completely embedded in the reason for The Growth's existence. Where I thought Kevin was most important was with regards to his relationship with Tax. It allowed for an odd couple relationship which I find always works well. Building their exploits to the point where they both changed each other for the better was one of the prouder aspects of the story for me and still brings me great pleasure. I enjoyed constructing the world's biggest chance of survival being somewhat of a physically weak coward. Albeit one who forces himself forward on a journey of redemption. We have to remember that for every Tax there are ninety-nine normal people whose reflex action would always be to run and hide. We're not all immediately heroic. That's why when we catch up with a stranded Kevin he is physically and mentally damaged by the journey he had been on. Killing is an unnatural thing for normal, modern men, and I wanted to reflect this in the toll it took on Kevin.

Emma is named after my dear sister. She is the kind of inclusive character I really wanted to write into the story running parallel to Kevin and Tax's exploits. I saw her as a force for good but burdened by the ghosts of her past. Emma had to fight her whole life to be taken seriously in a male focused sport and this overlapped into her personal life where she was under constant attack for being in love with a woman. Her arc is one akin to the phoenix rising from the flames. Just like Tax, when all seems hopeless, Emma finds a path of good to throw one hundred percent at. I wanted Emma to be a fighter in every sense and although it was close at times, it was nice to see her come out swinging.

Michael was fun to write because I wanted a vile villain who had no redeeming qualities. With the other characters I tried to balance them to be more realistic in that they were normal people with flaws. Michael, however, was someone I wanted to be almost theatrical in his villainy. We read how he lost his mind in that attic over his financial and personal stresses, and this is important to make that leap into fanatical religious behaviour. The reader knows The Growth is a product of

The Growth

science and not religion which makes Michael's murderous cult more heinous. How many hide behind religion to kill? What gave Michael the right? I wanted him to frustrate and get under the skin of the reader, so they longed for retribution. He represents a collective of men that Emma has battled with her whole life so it was fitting she would be my "cult buster."

You will have noticed the title of these notes and I'll go a little into that now. While the Cursed trilogy was a product of isolation brought on by lockdown, The Growth was based on my contempt for how large portions of society behaved during those difficult times. The news reports and governmental updates which appear sporadically throughout the book were my cynical view of how I think things would go should such a creature ooze out of the sewer. Those early days of lockdown were particularly disheartening as supermarket shelves were ransacked because people began to selfishly stockpile. My first visit to the shops had been like taking part in a riot. The more ignorant the shopper, the more they got. It was a moment to help one another but instead the most vulnerable were soon getting left behind. My youngest daughter was still in nappies at the time and queuing outside a shop while wondering if I'd get any seemed unfairly stressful. Of course, these are First World problems, but the selfishness was sobering.

The flipside to all the negativity is while

The Growth

the government postured, the real heroes stepped up. Maybe it was because people had more time, but it was heartening to see displays of kindness from neighbour to neighbour. The NHS here was nothing short of heroic as the death toll flashed across the bottom of our television screens. Those frontline workers deserved the nation applauding them but not instead of the pay rise our government was so hellbent on denying them. It's particularly distressing to note that the government had been in the process of dismantling our national health service shortly before COVID struck. I wonder how many lives would have been saved if the service hadn't been poorly treated prior to the pandemic. Anyway, I digress, and so reluctantly step down from my soap box. The point is The Growth simply showed the world what it truly was at its core. There will always be people like Michael trying to change the narrative to fit their own ideals and there will always be those in power trying to profit from the misery.

So, why re-release the duology as one book? As well as the reasons stated earlier in this ramble, there is one truth. The only negative feedback I had about either book was that it was too short. Doing this edition has allowed me to right a wrong so I am able to move forward with other projects. The Growth always nagged at me and burned at my heels. It deserves my attention before I

The Growth

(hopefully) progress to new heights. Both books were originally conceived in 2021 and published in 2022 and although that doesn't seem so long ago, my writing has improved somewhat since then. I owed it to myself and any potential readers to tweak and rework the original texts to bring it screaming into 2024. Thankfully, a complete rewrite wasn't necessary otherwise I think I would have gone insane and locked myself in the attic like Michael. Another cool aspect of this edition is being able to work with the same team who helped bring Below Economic Thresholds and Not a Good Fit at This Time to life. I'm of course talking about the talented editing and formatting skills of Damien Casey (a great writer in his own right) and Laura Cathcart aka Cut Fingers for producing incredible cover and interior art.

The author notes for my debut collection (Not a Good Fit at This Time) were greatly received and I hope the same will be said for the above rather than people assuming I've disappeared up my own backside. I just want to thank you all for taking time to read my work as it really does blow my mind. I'm a working-class writer who takes nothing for granted so please know it means the absolute world to me. Be safe out there, dear reader because it might not be the creature who seeks to cause you the most harm.

The Growth

-Adam Hulse March 2024

Printed in Great Britain
by Amazon